THE ART OF WILLIAM MORRIS

IN CROSS STITCH

THE ART OF WILLIAM MORRIS IN CROSS STITCH

Barbara Hammet

Reader's Digest

THE READER'S DIGEST ASSOCIATION, INC.

Pleasantville, New York / Montreal

A READER'S DIGEST BOOK
Edited and published by David & Charles Ltd.

First published in the UK in 1996

Library of Congress Cataloging in Publication Data

Hammet, Barbara.
    The art of William Morris in cross stitch : over 40 projects
inspired by the design master/Barbara Hammet.
      p.   cm.
    Includes index.
    ISBN 0-89577-886-6
    1. Cross-stitch—Patterns. 2. Canvas embroidery—Patterns.
3. Decoration and ornament—England. 4. Morris, William,
1834-1896. I. Title.
TT778.C76H353 1996
746.44'3041—dc20
                                               96-2978
                                                CIP

Line drawings by Barbara Hammet
Photography by Tim Hill
Styling by Zöe Hill
Book design by Maggie Aldred
Reader's Digest and the Pegasus logo are registered trademarks of The Reader's
Digest Association, Inc.

Printed in Italy

Contents

Introduction

illiam Morris was one of those rare designers whose name instantly evokes a recognizable style, familiar to people around the world. He was an extraordinary man, who not only theorized about the way things should be but tried to make them happen. In the process, he became a master of pattern making, stained-glass design and technique, tile painting, tapestry, weaving, carpet making, fine printing, and bookbinding. He revived the art of vegetable dyeing and altered the course of interior decoration and decorative art. He became an expert in the history of textiles, wrote poetry and stories, translated Norse sagas, lectured on design, campaigned for the preservation of the character of medieval churches, and made a significant contribution to the socialist movement. When he died, his doctor commented that he had achieved enough for 10 men. In THE ART OF WILLIAM MORRIS IN CROSS STITCH, I have tried to capture his diverse skills, drawing not only on his printed designs but also on his woven fabrics, wallpapers, tapestries, and embroideries, and on the fine books he produced at the end of his life.

William Morris was born in 1834, the oldest son of a prosperous family. He spent his boyhood at Woodford Hall in Epping Forest in eastern England. His father, a stockbroker, made a fortunate investment in a mining company, which provided William with a comfortable private income as a young man. At Oxford University, where he was studying for the church, he met Edward Burne-Jones, a fellow theology student, who became a lifelong friend and colleague. Both men decided to concentrate on art rather than religion and chose other

William Morris provided a wealth of inspiration in his designs and in his approach.

careers. Morris began to study architecture, while Burne-Jones moved to London to study painting under Dante Gabriel Rossetti, a bohemian poet and painter and founder member of the new Pre-Raphaelite Brotherhood, which was devoted to re-creating an art of medieval intensity. When the architect's office where Morris worked moved to London, the friends were reunited, and Morris came under the influence of Rossetti, who persuaded him to give up architecture in favor of painting.

It was Rossetti who organized a group of artists to paint frescoes in the new Oxford Union building, and Morris joined in, painting a scene from the legends of King Arthur. During this time in Oxford, he met Jane Burden

The Red House.

(Janey). Rossetti was always looking for beautiful women to model for him, and Janey, with her striking face, melancholy expression, and abundant dark hair, fitted the description. Both he and Morris were strongly attracted to her, and it was a shock to Morris's friends when he asked her to marry him. Since she was a working-class girl, the child of a stable worker, it was a socially unacceptable match, and Morris's family did not attend the wedding.

William Morris married Janey in 1859 and asked his friend Philip Webb to design them a house. Called the Red House because it was built from red brick instead of stone, in the style of Kent country building, Webb's creation was more like a large cottage than the usual gentleman's residence. However, it was spacious,

with high-ceilinged rooms, plain brickwork, and a massive oak staircase. From the outside, it had a picturesque Gothic appearance.

Morris devised a decorative scheme to suit the new house, one that included objects made by him, his family, and his friends. Influenced by the Oxford scheme, the drawing room was decorated with scenes from the Arthurian legends, for which Morris himself painted birds and trees in the style of old tapestry. Gradually over a period of time embroidered hangings, stained-glass windows, tiles, furniture, metalwork, and glassware were added.

William Morris and Janey were happy in those early years. Their two daughters were born at the Red House — Jenny in 1861 and May the following year. Groups of friends frequently spent weekends there and enthusiastically joined in the decorating. Regular visitors were Edward Burne-Jones and his wife, Georgina, Rossetti and his wife, Lizzie, Philip Webb, the painters Ford Maddox Brown and Arthur Hughes, Charles Faulkner and his sister Kate, who later designed for the company, the poet Algernon Charles Swinburne, and Janey's sister Bessy, a skilled embroiderer. There was plenty of food and wine, good humor, and practical jokes. More seriously, it began to occur to them that others might like to be able to buy similar things, and gradually the notion of a business devoted to high-class decorative art took shape.

This concern began as a cooperative in which Morris was to organize the work and ask the others for designs as necessary. It was called Morris, Marshall, Faulkner and Co. and was located in Red Lion Square in London. Its early work was mainly designing stained glass and embroidery for churches, but gradually more crafts were added to the repertoire, and Morris was increasingly involved with the designing. After a few years, some of the original members dropped out, and Morris re-formed the company as Morris and Co.

By this time the family had regretfully given up the Red House so that Morris could be closer to his work. They lived in several houses in London over the years. But the only other house he felt deeply attached to was Kelmscott Manor, on the upper reaches of the River Thames, although it held dark memories for him. In 1871 he rented it jointly with Rossetti, supposedly as a country home but really as a discreet place for Janey and Rossetti to be together without causing unnecessary scandal. In 1867 Rossetti had asked her to model for him again, and an intense and, on his part, indiscreet relationship developed, with him painting adoring portraits and writing passionate poetry.

While Rossetti was at Kelmscott, William went on long trips to Iceland, pursuing his latest enthusiasm, the Norse sagas. Rossetti's behavior became very difficult and culminated in a breakdown, causing the relationship to peter out. For the Morris family, life went on. But Janey was often an invalid; and William, blaming himself for having failed to make her happy, redirected his energy into his work, which was earning him a substantial reputation.

Interior design as well as individual patterns spread his influence because the effects he produced were so different from the fussiness and clutter of the contemporary English Victorian style. Visiting homes he lived in makes me realize how much we still strive for the effects he popularized. He even started the fashion for plain whitewashed walls. He described the basic necessities thus: "First a book-case with a great many books in it; next a table that will keep steady when you write at it; then several chairs that you can move, and a bench that you can sit or lie upon; next a cupboard with drawers ... you will want pictures or engravings ... real works of art on the wall; or else the wall itself must be ornamented with some beautiful and restful pattern ... a vase or two to put flowers in, which latter you must have sometimes if you live in a town ... . A small carpet which can be bundled out of the room in two minutes will be useful." Usefulness and beauty were the two essentials, and he urged simplicity. "I have never been in any rich man's home that would not have looked the better for having a bonfire made outside it of nine-tenths of all it held," he said, adding that only the kitchen was likely to contain objects of any use at all.

The way things were conventionally done mattered little to Morris. He believed that the form of an object should evolve from the material it was made from and the function it was designed for. So before he could begin a design, he had to teach himself the techniques of working with the medium from scratch and evolve the design from an understanding of its strength and qualities. Ideally, he wanted an object to be the product of a close relationship between craftsman and product, with the craftsman putting something of his own imagination into the process. He found these qualities in medieval craftsmanship, and they are essentially the characteristics of the Arts and Crafts movement that developed under his influence and went on to sweep through Europe and North America.

The style of pattern making Morris developed was very different from that which prevailed in the Victorian period, which favored realistically modeled posies in a harsh colors. Although Morris used nature for inspiration, he was brimming with enthusiasm for the patterns he found in the medieval manuscripts he collected and the tapestry and embroidery he admired. Thus he worked much more with flat shapes in decorative arrangements. I find this quality most interesting, and it is the one that has inspired most of the embroidery designs in this book. The more closely I studied the original designs, the more I admired his skill at arranging the patterns with the spaces between them – spaces that are made more prominent by the use of colored backgrounds. This is a quality I sought to capture in the embroidery. It makes for interesting abstract shapes even when only fragments of the pattern are actually chosen, as they are in the Flower Garden designs (see page 85–89).

He felt strongly that without structure a design had no meaning. He based his theories on an enthusiastic study of historic textiles, from which he evolved three main pattern types. All-over designs were formed by either "the branch formed on a diagonal line," which represented "the universal acceptance of con-

The Wild Tulip is an example of a Morris design based on a continuous diagonal branch.

tinuous growth," or "the net framed on variously proportioned diamonds." To these he added "turn over" designs based on woven patterns.

He frequently used the continuous meandering diagonal branch on which three of the embroideries in the book are based — the Evenlode, Kennet, and Wild Tulip. Dealing with a continuous directional line in a small embroidery can be difficult, so with my adaptations of the Kennet and the Wild Tulip I have concentrated on the detail between the diagonal branches. Among the designs I have adapted, the Wild Tulip is quite unusual in using a dark outline around the flowers. It is one of very few designs where I have made use of backstitch, which was the only way to capture the sinuousness of the shapes (see page 80).

Morris was very skillful at creating designs based on the network of diamonds. The Strawberry Thief is an excellent example. He posed his birds and his flowers so that they con-

The Strawberry Thief is designed around a subtle network of diamond shapes.

tributed to the complex and subtle network. The basic network of ogee-shaped diamonds is made up of the blue stems with the rounded leaves. I have included part of it in my adaptation (see page 12). On top of this structure is laid a framework of diagonal chevron shapes, one of which follows the line of the bird's tail down through its forward leg. The effect of all these swirls and diagonals is to make a very dynamic, lively image.

To these forms Morris added his distinctive "turn over" designs, based on his study of the patterns dictated by the weaving technique. These use pairs of animals or flowers in mirror image, usually arranged one above another. Examples I have used are the Dove and Rose and Brer Rabbit designs (pages 30 and 110).

Morris's first experiment with off-the-shelf

repeating designs, to fill the gap between the big commissions, was with wallpaper. He hoped to be able to print it himself but quickly found that was too difficult, so he entrusted the job to a company that still used the craft technique of printing from wooden blocks. Next, he tried printing on fabric, again wanting to have control of the whole process. Most commercial mills were using the new chemical dyes and printing with machines that had the design engraved on the rollers. This was quick and economical, but it produced harshly colored goods that had no individuality and that faded unpredictably. Together with Thomas Wardle, a manufacturer who was an enthusiast for traditional methods, Morris set about re-establishing the traditional dyeing arts, going as far back as the medieval herbal books for recipes. In those days he was permanently blue in color from being up to his elbows in indigo dye; when he visited his friends, their servants sometimes tried to send him to the tradesman's entrance.

To create multicolored designs, Morris selected a variety of natural materials. For red, he used both madder and bark and cochineal and kermes. For blue, he used indigo and woad. Yellow was made from weld (wild mignonette), bark, and hedge plants like poplar, birch, and broom. Brown came from walnut roots. Other colors were obtained by superimposing one color on another. The complexity made the printing process a slow one but one that Morris felt added character to the design as well as giving him a variety of reliable colors that would not distort as they faded.

Merton Abbey on the River Wandle became Morris's headquarters after 1881. He moved all his workshops there — stained glass, weaving, tapestry making, and carpet production, as well as dyeing and printing. The river water was used for dyeing and washing the cloth, and the meadows were spread with multicolored fabric drying in the sun — a perfect setting for Morris to realize his ambition to create what he called the "art which is made by the people and for the people, as a happiness to the maker and the user." He was prepared to use machinery where it would speed production without reducing the operator to a mere machine minder. He approved of "the old machine, the improved tool, which is auxiliary to the man and only works as long as his hand is thinking."

Looms were regarded as tools, even the modern Jacquard loom he brought over from France, along with a weaver to teach him the technique. In creating woven cloth, he could indulge his love of rich texture as well as pattern. He used a wide variety of threads — wool, mohair, linen, silk, cotton, and combinations of these. It is easy to forget that even the printed fabrics were often silk or velveteen, not just the cotton of most modern reprintings. To try to recapture some of this richness, I have included designs in which a variety of different textured threads are used—not perhaps the threads Morris was familiar with, but modern threads that give a variety of sheen and reflectivity to the colors, interpreting the effects he obtained.

Tapestry and embroidery both made important contributions to the company's work. Morris had taught himself to weave tapestries with the help of old manuals. Good tapestry, he thought, should rival the best painting but not imitate it. His kind of tapestry would seek inspiration from the golden age of tapestry production — the medieval. He set up a loom in his bedroom, and his diaries record how he fitted the acquisition of this new skill into his busy life. "Up at five: three and a half hours' tapestry." This was followed by a full day's work.

Embroidery was also important from the start. As the company's business became more

The Dove and Rose is one of Morris's distinctive "turn over" designs.

domestic, the focus became pillows, fire screens, and door and bed curtains. These could be embroidered for the customer or supplied as outline kits for the ladies to embroider themselves — a relatively inexpensive way to acquire a prestigious work by Morris and Co.

William Morris died on October 3, 1896, having achieved much and in many spheres. The cause of death was complications resulting from diabetes. His body was taken from London by train to be buried at Kelmscott. The oak coffin, decorated with a wreath of bay leaves, was carried to the church on an open farm cart decked with branches of vine and willow.

Morris left us a wealth of inspiration in his designs and in his approach to the arts. The maxim he laid down for embroidery could be applied to any craft: "There is no excuse for doing anything which is not strikingly beautiful."

The Bird Pillows

These three embroideries are based on William Morris's Strawberry Thief, Bird, and Woodpecker textiles to make a trio of throw pillows with a common ornithological theme. In each case I have centered the embroidery design on the bird. Framing the bird with a leaf border is a formula I worked out to unify the three designs. It helps to preserve the feeling of intense pattern all over, which is an attribute of the original designs, while focusing attention on the selected area. Each bird embroidery has a border made up of leaves characteristic of that particular design.

Morris's textiles are united by dark backgrounds and similar color schemes, but they were produced by three quite different techniques. The Strawberry Thief design was a printed fabric. The Bird was a heavy woven woolen double cloth. And the Woodpecker was a handwoven tapestry.

The Strawberry Thief was inspired by a specific and rather commonplace occurrence at Kelmscott Manor. One day Morris watched thrushes find their way under the netting to plunder his strawberry crop. He had made a deliberate study of birds some time before and included them in a series of designs, including the Bird weave. So he would have watched the destruction of his fruit in a philosophical spirit as he wondered whether he could make use of the experience. The Strawberry Thief chintz is

Three pillow designs (clockwise from left): *Woodpecker, Strawberry Thief, and Bird.*

one of his most original designs and has proved to be one of his most enduringly popular. It is a splendid example of the way Morris contrived to combine his natural observation with the underlying geometric structure he favored in his designs. The profusion of flowers and leaves, even the stance of the birds, are all arranged to form a complex interlocking network of diamond shapes.

The heavy woolen Bird fabric was one of Morris's favorites. He chose to hang it around the walls in his drawing room, where with its subdued colors and rich pattern it gave a very medieval effect, as though the room were hung with tapestries. It was the first of the Morris designs that I chose to adapt for cross stitch, attracted as I was to the fabric and particularly to the combination of bird and willow branch with its beautifully shaped leaves.

All the Morris designs show more than one bird, and in this one as in the Strawberry Thief, the birds face one another in pairs. To do justice to the detail and pattern of the original birds, I realized I could include only a single example in a pillow-sized design. My first version of the design worked all the leaves in blue, as in the original, where Morris relied on the contrast of the sinuous willow leaves with the much stronger, more angular ones to give enough variety. However, looking at the three pillows together, I decided to vary the shade of blue and introduce the green into the bottom leaf and the marigold leaf at the top in order to have more colors common to all three designs. The border is composed of details from the willow branches.

The Woodpecker tapestry (right) is a an unusual piece of work without the repeating pattern elements of the other two. It shows a tree laden with fruit in which sit a woodpecker and another bird. Around the trunk twine enormous acanthus leaves, and growing up

around it are periwinkles, marigolds, tulips, and other flowers. There is no regular pattern, but the whole area is filled in a very decorative way, with equal emphasis all over the design. It is bordered by twining honeysuckle on the left

Morris's Woodpecker tapestry differs from the Bird and Strawberry Thief designs in its lack of regular patterning. For the Woodpecker pillow the background has been simplified and attention focused on the woodpecker.

and right, and an inscription at top and bottom taken from one of Morris's poems about a legendary Italian king, Picus, who was changed into a woodpecker.

In this design I have focused on the top part of the tree with the woodpecker and surrounding leaves and fruit. I find that there is something very traditional and satisfying about an image of a bird in a tree. Once an area has been chosen, it is often necessary to simplify and adapt to make it fit into the required shape. Here, for example, I took the acanthus leaf that Morris put behind the tree trunk and used it in front to fill the left corner and direct attention back to the center of the design. Wherever my design had a gap, I chose a simple blue star-shaped flower from another part of the tapestry to fill it.

In all these designs, not only is the fabric used as a dark background to contrast with the predominantly light colors of the birds and the plants, but it is left void to provide an outline that delineates wings, feathers, eyes, and petals. In the Woodpecker design, it is also used as dark vertical shading on the leaves, in imitation of the tapestry technique Morris used. I have chosen to extend the technique to the trunk on which the woodpecker perches, which Morris wove in brown. I have simply outlined it because I felt the three designs would have greater unity if each of the three featured its bird against a dark background.

The leaves I have used for the border of the Woodpecker design are based on the leaves of the periwinkle around the base of the trunk in Morris's original design. I picked them because their strong, sharp shapes reminded me of the woodpecker's beak and his vigorous character. The colored bands that surround the borders of all three designs were suggested by the ones Morris used to outline the borders on the tapestry.

Strawberry Thief, Bird, and Woodpecker

FINISHED SIZE: 14 x 14in (36 x 36cm)
STITCH COUNT: 200 x 200

MATERIALS FOR EACH PILLOW
18 x 18in (46 x 46cm) of 14-count Aida in navy
Stranded floss as listed in the keys on pages 17, 19, and 21
Size 24 tapestry needle
15in (38cm) pillow form
Backing fabric to match

1. Press the fabric. A frame is recommended for this design, though it is not essential. If you do decide to manage without a frame, bear in mind that the continuous stitching of the bands of color around the borders will tend to pull the material in. You can allow for this by consciously working the bands at a loose tension.
2. Mark the central horizontal and vertical guidelines with basting (see page 118). Because these are quite large and complex designs, I recommend marking lines of basting at the 20th, 40th, 60th, and 80th squares of the fabric (left and right, top and bottom) so that you can keep checking your position.
3. The design is stitched with two strands of stranded floss throughout. Begin by working the bird; complete it before going on to stitch the flowers and foliage.
4. When you get to the borders, it is natural to turn the work so that the part being worked is closest to you. If you do that, you need to be careful to keep the direction of your stitching consistent with the rest of the work.
5. Finally check carefully for details omitted, remove the guidelines, and press (see page 119).

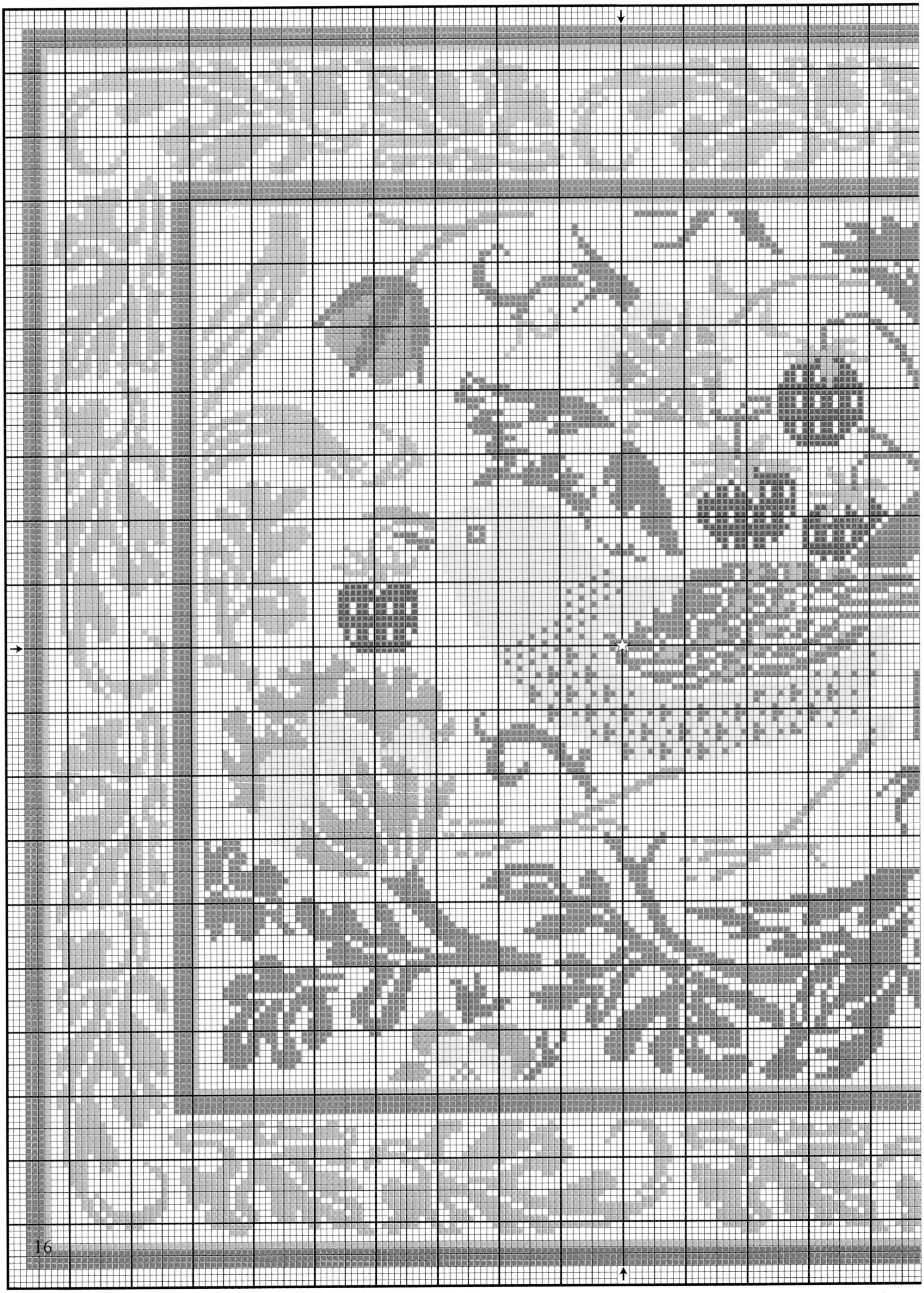

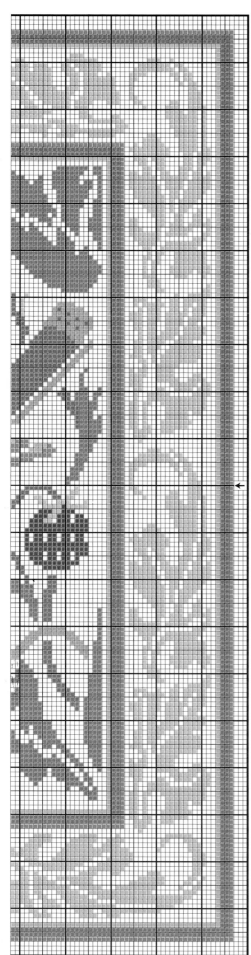

STRAWBERRY THIEF

ANCHOR

215

161

160

011

338

337

362

278

301

☆
Middle point

7. To make the finished embroidery into a pillow, see page 123. Alternatively, frame the design if you prefer (see page 122).

STRAWBERRY THIEF KEY

Color	Anchor	DMC	Madeira
Pale blue	160 (4)	827 (4)	1002 (3)
Darker blue	161 (2)	813 (2)	1003 (2)
Green	215 (2)	3816 (2)	1702 (1)
Yellow	301 (1)	744 (1)	112 (1)
Yellow ocher	362 (1)	437 (1)	2012 (1)
Peach	337 (1)	3778 (1)	403 (1)
Rust	338 (2)	356 (2)	402 (1)
Lime	278 (1)	3819 (1)	1414 (1)
Red	011 (1)	351 (1)	406 (1)

The design was stitched with Anchor threads. The alternatives may not be exact color equivalents. Quantities are shown in parentheses.

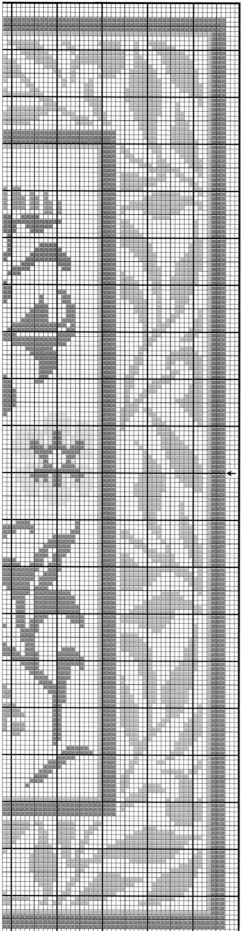

BIRD

ANCHOR

215

161

160

338

337

362

278

301

☆
Middle point

BIRD KEY

Color	Anchor	DMC	Madeira
Pale blue	160 (4)	827 (4)	1002 (3)
Darker blue	161 (2)	813 (2)	1003 (2)
Green	215 (1)	3816 (1)	1702 (1)
Yellow	301 (1)	744 (1)	112 (1)
Yellow ocher	362 (1)	437 (1)	2012 (1)
Peach	337 (1)	3778 (1)	403 (1)
Rust	338 (2)	356 (2)	402 (1)
Lime	278 (2)	3819 (2)	1414 (1)

The design was stitched using Anchor threads. The alternatives may not be exact color equivalents. Quantities are shown in parentheses.

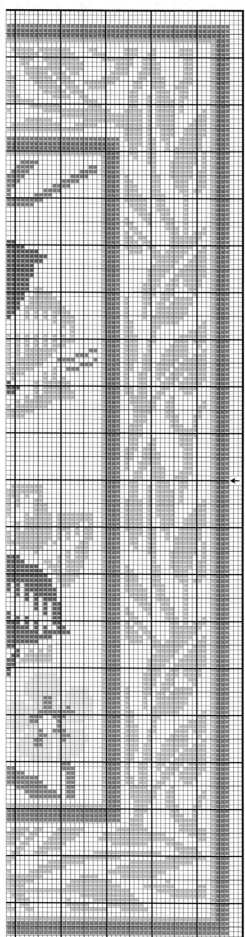

WOODPECKER

ANCHOR

216

214

161

160

338

336

278

301

☆
Middle point

WOODPECKER KEY

Color	Anchor	DMC	Madeira
Pale blue	160 (4)	827 (4)	1002 (3)
Darker blue	161 (2)	813 (2)	1003 (2)
Green	216 (2)	3815 (2)	1703 (2)
Lighter green	214 (1)	3817 (1)	1702 (1)
Yellow	301 (1)	744 (1)	112 (1)
Peach	336 (1)	758 (1)	403 (1)
Rust	338 (2)	356 (2)	402 (1)
Lime	278 (2)	3819 (2)	1414 (1)

The design was stitched using Anchor threads. The alternatives may not be exact color equivalents. Quantities are shown in parentheses.

Violets
Bed Linen

This project shows you how to use up some of the pieces of white Aida that all embroiderers accumulate. With it you can make an attractive nightgown bag entwined with violets and a matching decoration for a pillowcase. For this design I took my inspiration from Morris's Blackthorn design, which brims over with flowers of all sorts — branches of blackthorn with starry white flowers and fierce thorns, nodding fritillaries, wood anemones and violets, orange daisies and long, toothed leaves. Although it seems to overflow with flowers, they are in fact formed into a symmetrical, carefully organized pattern against a dark green background that gives the design an atmosphere of the wildwood.

I selected the violet motifs from beneath the blackthorn tree because they were symmetrical, quite delicate, and small scale, and would stand alone without the surrounding patterns. I thought the heart shapes made by the stems were attractive and appropriate. Morris frequently formed his plants into heart shapes. In the language of flowers, popular with the Victorians, the violet symbolizes love, but I think Morris would have used the shape simply to echo and accentuate the heart-shaped leaves of the violets.

The dark background of the original, which was necessary for contrast with the white flowers of the blackthorn, was not essential for the violet motifs and not suitable for decorating white linen; in my adaptation, the violets look fresh and airy against plain white.

Violets Pillow Band (left) *and Nightgown Bag* (right).

Violets Nightgown Bag

Design size: 6 x 11in (15 x 28cm)

Finished size of bag: 10½ x 13½ in
(27 x 34cm)

Stitch count: 169 x 86

Materials

12 x 16in (30 x 41cm) 16-count Aida
in white
Stranded floss as listed in the
key on page 27
Size 26 tapestry needle
Lace edging, about 27in (70cm), to match
pillowcase
¾ yd (69cm) violet fabric to make the
case outer and lining
Matching sewing thread
15 x 31in (38 x 80cm) 2oz (50g) batting
40in (102cm) purple ribbon for ties

1. Mark the central horizontal and vertical guidelines with basting (see page 118).

2. Begin at the center, with the darkest green. Using two strands over one block of the fabric, work the central leaf.

3. Continue with the interlaced stems, counting carefully as you go.

4. Embroider the violets and the other leaves.

5. When you have finished, remove the guidelines and press (see page 119).

6. Following the pattern shown in Fig. 1, cut out the violet fabric for pieces A, B, C, and D; and the batting for pieces B and C. It would be helpful to make paper patterns.

7. Stitching lines for the Aida are indicated on the chart. Mark the line on the Aida with basting. Sew the top of the Aida to the longer side of the back piece A, matching centers. Press the seam open.

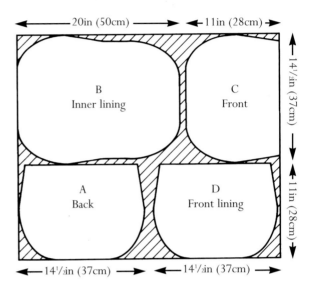

Fig. 1 Diagram for cutting lining fabric.

8. Place the Aida piece on lining piece B, right sides together. Place both pieces on top of the large piece of basting. Pin together around the Aida flap.

9. Cut the purple ribbon in half. Insert one piece so that it lies between the Aida and the lining. Let one end protrude from the center of the edge so that it will be stitched in the seam (see Fig. 2). Stitch around the flap, following the line indicated on the chart.

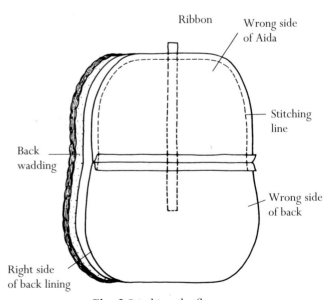

Fig. 2 Stitching the flap.

10. Trim, turn, and press the flap. Place lace on top around the extreme edge of the Aida. Finish the ends and machine stitch in place, using white thread on top of the machine and violet in the bobbin.

11. Now fold the finished flap over and verify that the shape of the bag part reflects the shape of the flap, and that the sides taper in so that the stitching line meets the edge of the flap. It is nice to let the violet show through the lace a little at the sides. Adjust if necessary.

12. To the right side of the back and its batting, pin the right side of the front and its batting as shown in Fig. 3 (with the top edge of the front turned down over the batting). Stitch through the back batting, back, front and front batting. Leave the back lining free.

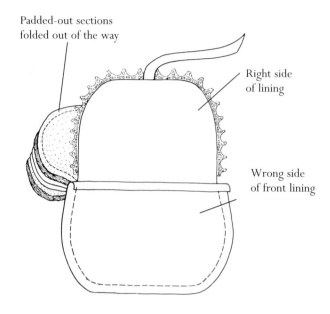

Padded-out sections folded out of the way

Right side of lining

Wrong side of front lining

Fig. 4 Finishing the lining.

15. Stitch the remaining piece of ribbon to the front to fasten the bag, hiding the turned-under raw edge with the stitching.

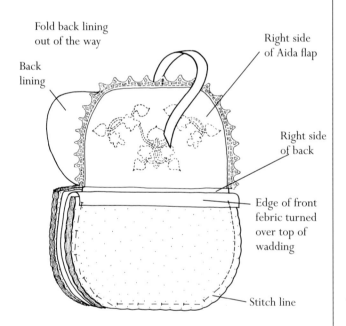

Fold back lining out of the way

Back lining

Right side of Aida flap

Right side of back

Edge of front febric turned over top of wadding

Stitch line

Fig. 3 Constructing the bag.

13. To the right side of the back lining, pin the right side of the front lining, with the top edge turned toward you. Stitch (see Fig. 4).

14. Trim and turn the padded front over the lining. Slipstitch the top edge of the front to the front lining.

The Violet motif.

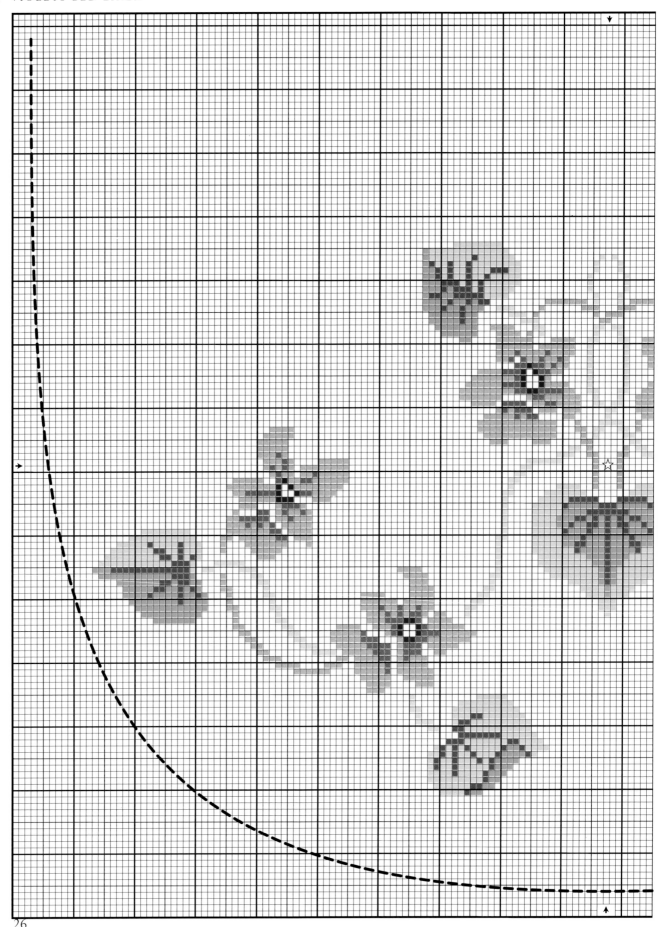

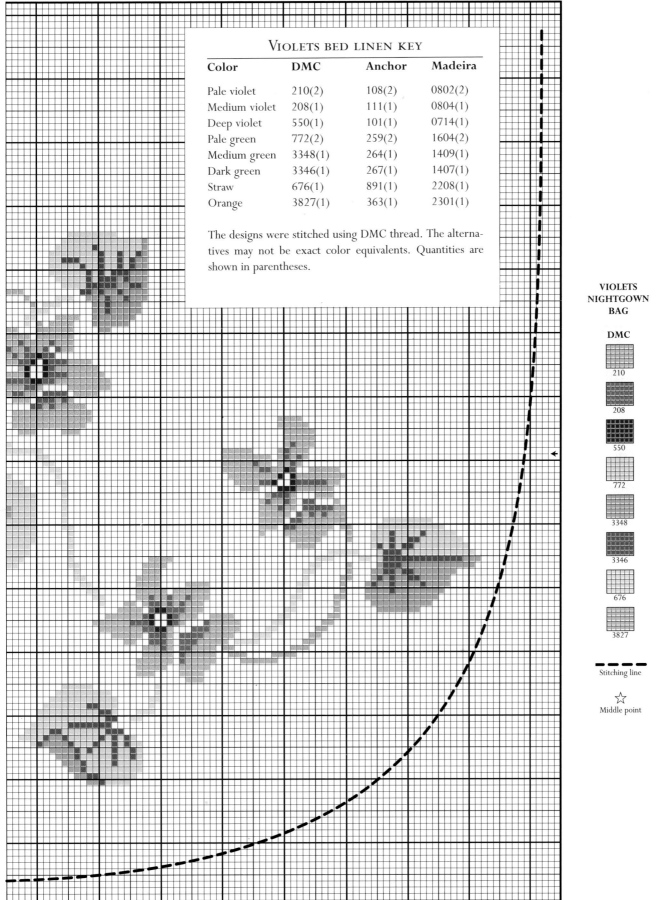

VIOLETS BED LINEN KEY

Color	DMC	Anchor	Madeira
Pale violet	210(2)	108(2)	0802(2)
Medium violet	208(1)	111(1)	0804(1)
Deep violet	550(1)	101(1)	0714(1)
Pale green	772(2)	259(2)	1604(2)
Medium green	3348(1)	264(1)	1409(1)
Dark green	3346(1)	267(1)	1407(1)
Straw	676(1)	891(1)	2208(1)
Orange	3827(1)	363(1)	2301(1)

The designs were stitched using DMC thread. The alternatives may not be exact color equivalents. Quantities are shown in parentheses.

VIOLETS NIGHTGOWN BAG

DMC

210

208

550

772

3348

3346

676

3827

– – – –
Stitching line

☆
Middle point

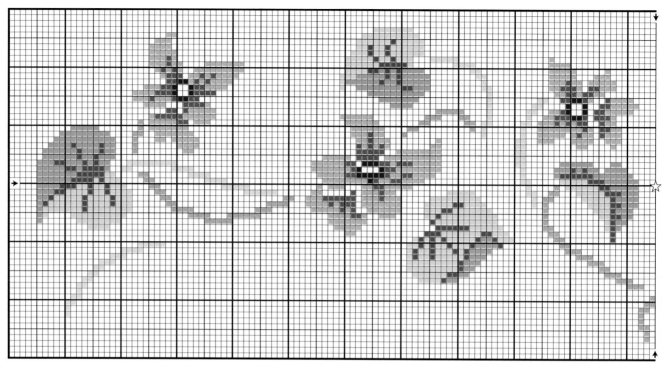

VIOLETS PILLOW BAND

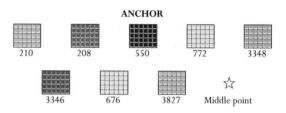

ANCHOR

210	208	550	772	3348
3346	676	3827	☆ Middle point	

Violets Pillow Band

DESIGN SIZE: 4in (10cm) band to fit a pillowcase
STITCH COUNT: 220 x 59

MATERIALS
8 x 20in (20 x 50cm) 16-count Aida in white
Stranded floss as listed in the
key on page 27
Size 26 tapestry needle
Narrow violet ribbon to cover the edges
of the Aida, or ribbon and lace made to
thread ribbon through
Ready-made white cotton pillowcase—the
one illustrated is ruffled with 4¼yd (3.9m)
narrow white edging lace added
Matching sewing thread

1. Mark the central horizontal and vertical guidelines with basting (see page 118).

2. Work the embroidery, using two strands over one block of the fabric. Start and finish lengths of floss securely, since the pillowcase will get a lot of washing and wear. Try not to take lengths of floss over spaces.

3. When you have finished, remove the guidelines and press (see page 119).

4. Pin the ribbon, or lace with ribbon threaded through, on each side of the design, leaving a 4in (10cm) strip in between. Machine stitch along the embroidery side of the ribbon. Trim the fabric carefully so that the edge will be hidden under the ribbon.

5. Undo the side seams of the pillowcase about 8in (20cm). Fold the back of the pillowcase out of the way. Matching the center with the center of the short side of the pillowcase, pin the

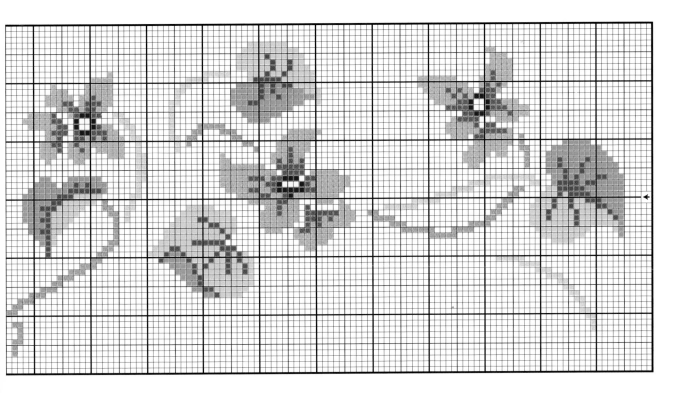

embroidered band about 2in (5cm) in from the edge (see Fig. 5). Stitch along the outside edges of the ribbon. It is advisable to stitch both edges of the ribbon from the same direction.

6. Remove the guidelines and restitch the side seams to complete. Press (see page 119).

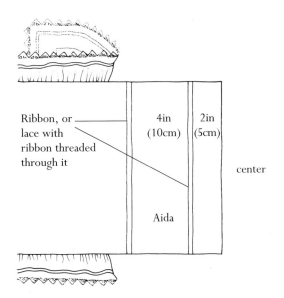

Ribbon, or lace with ribbon threaded through it

4in (10cm)

2in (5cm)

center

Aida

Fig. 5 Applying the embroidery to the pillowcase.

Variations

1. The embroidery could be worked on 32-count Belfast linen worked over two threads to give exactly the same size, or on 14-count Aida, which would give a slightly larger size.

2. Work the design for the pillowcase on a 4-in-wide (10cm) Aida band with a damask edge, repeating the design as often as you wish.

3. Use the design charted above on guest towels, applied in a similar way to the pillowcase.

4. The central violets motif from the nightgown bag design could be embroidered over waste canvas (see page 116) onto the pocket of a bath robe.

5. The nightgown bag design could be stitched at each end of a dresser scarf or table runner.

The Dove and Rose Picture

his quietly charming picture would add a touch of tradition to any room. The soft colors gently echo the message of peace and restfulness, which is also symbolized by the two doves with their olive branch. When creating it, I imagined it mounted and framed, and hung perhaps in a hallway to help give a gracious welcome to visitors as they arrive. Initially I chose a mount in gray-green but decided I needed a warmer colour and found a remnant of red upholstery fabric that seemed just right.

The central design of this piece is taken from William Morris's Dove and Rose, a woven silk and wool double cloth of some complexity. I concentrated on the main features — the doves, the olive branch, and the roses — and worked them into a rectangular design, which I liked but did not feel was fully resolved. Coming back to it later, I decided to highlight the symbolic meaning of the design by accentuating the message of peace. Remembering that Renaissance painters used a circular format for their most peaceful images of the Madonna and Child, I decided to try that. It was pleasing but left empty spaces — hence the addition of the message "Peace Be In This House".

Morris himself frequently added text to his embroideries and tapestries. His earliest known embroidery, when he was still teaching himself the craft, used the motto "If I can" as part of a large and ambitious repeating design with birds and trees, fully embroidered in wools on linen.

Who but William Morris would choose that as his first project? As he grew older, the messages became longer, often including his poetry. Although he did not incorporate any words into this particular design, I felt that it would not be departing from his style to do so myself.

Morris's Dove and Rose has a particularly attractive texture, for sometimes the wool, sometimes the silk, and sometimes a mixture of both appears, on the surface. To capture something of this effect, I have used a mixture of floss ton, pearl cotton, and blending filament against the matte background of fine ecru Aida. The original textile comes in a variety of colors and I have combined two of them to incorporate shades of beige, pink, dark green, and jade.

FINISHED SIZE: about 9in (23cm) diameter
STITCH COUNT: 160 x 160

MATERIALS
16 x 16in (41 x 41cm) 18-count
Aida in ecru
Size 26 tapestry needle
Stranded floss, pearl cotton, and blending
thread as listed in the key on page 33

1. Mark the central horizontal and vertical guidelines on the Aida with lines of basting (see page 118).
2. Begin at the center with the dark green floss. Using two strands over one block of fabric, work all the dark green around the center line.
3. The dark green outlines the bird and forms a kind of skeleton for the design. Embroider all the dark green areas, counting carefully as you go.
4. Fill in the colored areas of birds, leaves and roses. The darkest and lightest pinks are worked with two strands of stranded floss, as are the

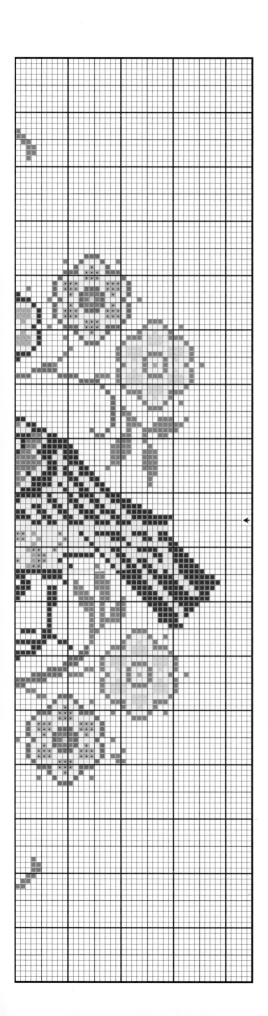

DOVE & ROSE

DMC

924

3768

992

760

754

760/4300

712 Perlé
No 12

☆
Middle
point

jade green and the dark gray-green. The middle pink is embroidered using a single strand of the darker pink with one of blending thread. The areas of pearl cotton are done with a single thread in No. 12 thickness.

5. The lettering is worked mainly in cross stitch, except for the small words, which are embroidered in backstitch with two strands of the dark green thread.

6. When you have finished, remove the guide-lines and press (see page 119).

7. I suggest framing this design in a square mat with a circular window of 10in (25cm). For framing instructions see page 122.

Variation

An alternative motto would be "Love Is Enough," taken from one of Morris's own poems. Arrange the phrase with "Love" at the top of the chart and "Is" centered above "Enough" at the bottom.

KEY

Color	DMC	Anchor	Madeira
Dark green	924 (2)	851 (2)	1706 (1)
Gray-green	3768 (1)	779 (1)	1707 (1)
Jade green	992 (1)	187 (1)	1202 (1)
Dark pink	760 (1)	1022 (1)	0405 (1)
Light pink	754 (1)	1012 (1)	0305 (1)
Medium pink	760/4300	1022/032	0405/000
	Blending thread (1)	Kreinik blending filament (1)	Rainbow blending thread (1)
Cream	712 Pearl No. 12 (1)	387 Pearl No. 12 (1)	

The embroidery was stitched using DMC stranded floss, metallic blending thread, and No. 12 pearl cotton. Alternatives are listed where they are available, but they are not exact color equivalents. Kreinik blending filament, for example, is thinner than the DMC or Madeira Rainbow blending threads and if you use this it may be necessary to use two threads together. Quantities are shown in parentheses.

Medieval Jewel Collection

This medieval-style jewel casket is based on one owned by William Morris's wife, Janey. It was a gift, made by the group of friends who helped to decorate the Red House. Hers is like a miniature treasure chest, bound in metal. I have copied the shape and interpreted the different textures by making the metal parts, which are dull and virtually black, out of charcoal gray yarn. The arched shapes are copied from Gothic detailing on the sides and the gold stitches represent the studs on the original. My casket hinges and opens in the same way as Janey Morris's, though that locked with a key. Mine is constructed from plastic canvas and lined with extra pieces of plastic canvas that have been quilted.

Both the shape and the fact that every wooden panel was covered with painted decoration reminded me of a medieval reliquary (a container for a saint's relics), particularly the sort covered in inlaid enamel work and gold. I knew I could not imitate the detail of the miniature paintings. So with the images of the reliquary and the treasure chest in mind, I decided to use fragments of Morris's Dragon and Peacock design to decorate the sides. I chose the dragons because in mythology it is their role to guard gold. And I interpreted them in metallic threads to capture the feeling of a treasure chest in which to keep precious objects.

Morris based his dragons on Oriental examples. In Chinese mythology, dragons fly through the skies chasing flaming pearls. And in his design, which I have followed, the heads are lower than the bodies, which twist around

above the heads and allow us to see the claws toward the top of the chart for the end pieces. Morris's design is for a woven wool fabric, a very largescale, grand design with a strong medieval feel. As was usual with his woven designs, he arranged both his dragons and peacocks in pairs, facing each other, which is a style particularly suitable for the weaving technique. I have copied this symmetrical style by using a pair of dragons facing each other. The chart for the side shows part of the body and the beginning of the wing. One section is a mirror image

The Medieval Jewel Casket and the jewels that accompany it (from left to right):
the Flower Pendant, the St. James Carnation Pendant, the Golden Bough Brooch, and the Silver Leaves Brooch.

of the other. The wings are continued in the decoration for the top flaps of the casket, which I have finished by repeating the Gothic detailing from the ends.

To fill the casket, I have designed four pieces of embroidered jewellery, all worked on a small scale. I had to buy a magnifying glass before I could attempt to sew the samples and was encouraged to find that with its help there was no difficulty.

One of the aims of Morris's company was to produce designs in metalwork, including jewel-ry. Although a number of drawings survive, very little was actually made; even so, Morris's style had a great impact on Art Nouveau jewel-ry. Burne-Jones was the most interested in this field, perhaps because his grandfather had been a jeweler. Not surprisingly, the group favored handmade pieces and a medieval style.

Jewel Casket

DESIGN SIZE: 6 x 4¹/₄ x 4¹/₄in
(15 x 11 x 11cm)

MATERIALS
Two sheets of 10-count plastic canvas,
preferably black or clear
Appleton's crewel yarn in charcoal grey
Madeira metallic No. 10 as listed in the
key on page 39
Madeira Glissen Gloss gold braid
Size 20 tapestry needle
Plastic curtain ring
6 x 4¹/₄in (15 x 11cm) black felt or
self-adhesive felt
9 x 22in (23 x 56cm) 2oz (56g) batting
27 x 36in (69 x 92cm) lining fabric (black
satin or similar)
Black sewing thread and needle
24in (61cm) very narrow braid or ribbon

1. Fig. 1 shows how to arrange the panels on the
plastic canvas. There is no need to cut them out
until they have been embroidered. Work two
ends, two sides, and two lids. The base is just
covered with felt.

2. The embroidery is worked in cross stitch,
using two strands of metallic thread together.
The charcoal gray wool is also used two strands
at a time for the cross stitched areas. Where it
is used to oversew edges and join pieces together it is used three strands at a time. The gold
braid is used singly.

3. When working with the metallic thread, use
reasonable lengths of thread; long pieces will
tend to shred. Try to keep ends out of the way.
If necessary, knot the end and leave it parked
outside the embroidered area until you have
finished, when it can be trimmed and threaded

through. If one of the two threads you are
working with suddenly gets shorter than the
other, try to find what has caught it and
straighten it out.

4. When you start the embroidery, do remember to leave a spare row all around the edge for
stitching the panels together. Work the gold
braid last, embroidering quite loosely and trying to keep it flat, at least on the front.

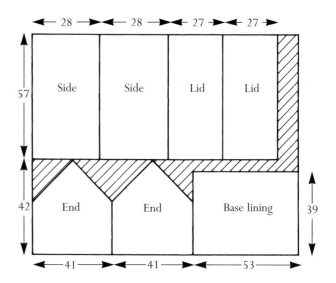

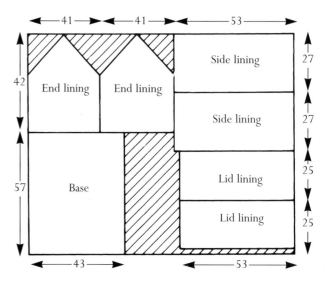

Numbers indicate number of plastic struts. Each sheet of
plastic canvas is 107 x 138 threads.

Fig. 1 Cutting diagram for plastic canvas.

5. To assemble casket, cut out all the pieces, remembering the extra row all round; use ordinary scissors. Cut off all the spiky bits to make a smooth edge. With the sloped ends first cut around a little way outside the line, cut in carefully to leave complete "steps."

6. Cut out the lining pieces as shown in Fig 1. Arrange them on the wadding and cut around them. Each piece will need covering with the lining fabric. Cut this out as well, leaving a 2in (5cm) margin all round for finishing off.

7. The spots on Fig. 2 indicate a quilting pattern. Mark the positions with a cross (use a felt-tip pen) on the back of the plastic canvas. Make a sandwich of lining fabric, batting, and plastic canvas. From the back, stitch the quilting by taking a small stitch through all thicknesses between the struts of the canvas. Bring the needle back through the same hole in the plastic canvas, a little away from the first stitch. Take the thread across the back to the next mark and repeat. Pull the thread tightly enough to create the quilted effect. Fasten off securely.

8. Turn over the edges of the lining fabric, mitering the corners neatly. Stitch in place, lacing across the back if necessary.

9. The casket opener is made from a curtain ring covered in buttonhole stitch (see page 121), worked in gold braid. Double another piece of gold braid and loop it through the ring. Bring the ends through the loop. Position the ring in the centre of the top edge of one of the lid pieces and stitch it to the back so that it projects by $^{3}/_{4}$ in (2 cm) from the top edge (see Fig. 3).

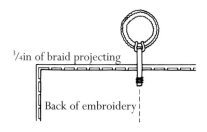

Fig. 3 Attaching the ring.

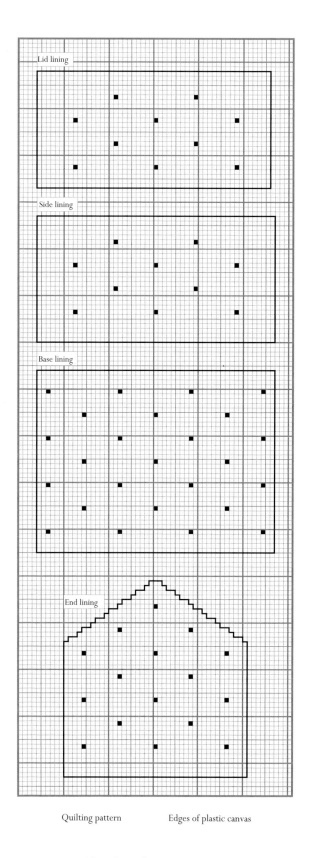

Quilting pattern   Edges of plastic canvas

Fig. 2 Quilting pattern.

10. Neaten the top edges of the end pieces of the embroidered panels by oversewing, using three strands of wool. This is the trickiest part. Normally one stitch goes through one hole, but add in extra stitches to cover the corners, and one for each side of the 'steps' (see Fig. 4).

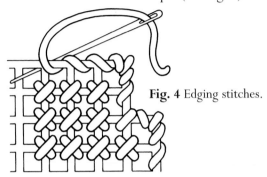

Fig. 4 Edging stitches.

11. Stitch the end lining piece to the wrong side of the embroidered plastic canvas along the top, over-sewing with sewing thread — the two pieces should be the same height. The edge will be neatened later by adding a narrow ribbon.

12. The lid lining pieces are located centrally on the plastic canvas pieces, and stitched all around. The sides are placed centrally, lined up with the bottom. There should be two struts left at each end and one at the top. Sew the lin-

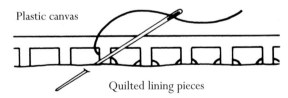

Fig. 5 Attaching the lining.

ings to the plastic canvas, leaving the bottom edges unstitched. Use black sewing thread and take tiny stitches through the edge of the lining fabric, then around the struts (see Fig. 5). On the short sides of the lid and side pieces the stitches will go through the charcoal gray cross stitched area, but will not show.

13. To sew the box together, begin by attaching one side to the base, using three strands of yarn, and overcasting. The side should sit on top of the

base. When you reach the end, place the end piece centrally on the end of the base (see Fig. 6). The end pieces sit inside the sides. Continue round the box. Sew up the sides.

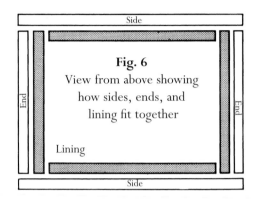

14. Oversew around the edges of the lid (see Fig. 4), missing two stitches in the middle of the uprights to allow for the "hinges," then along the top edges of the sides, leaving matching spaces.

15. Make hinges by overcasting in gold braid. Hide the ends under the quilted lining.

16. To finish the ends, open the casket out and invisibly stitch narrow ribbon along the short edge of the lid, over the gable end and along the edge of the other lid (see Fig. 7).

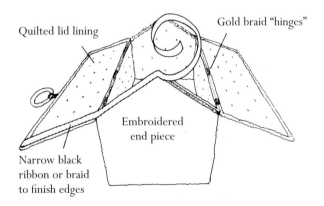

Fig. 7 Finishing the edges.

17. To finish, fit the quilted base inside. It does not need stitching. Turn the casket over and stitch the felt over the base, taking the stitches through the yarn covering the bottom edge.

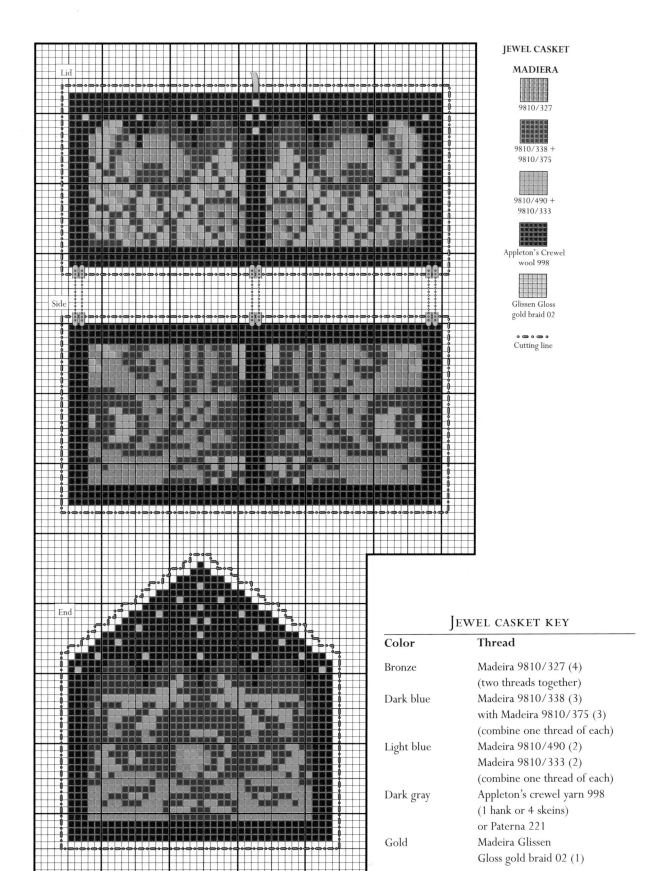

JEWEL CASKET

MADIERA

9810/327

9810/338 +
9810/375

9810/490 +
9810/333

Appleton's Crewel
wool 998

Glissen Gloss
gold braid 02

Cutting line

Lid

Side

End

JEWEL CASKET KEY

Color	Thread
Bronze	Madeira 9810/327 (4) (two threads together)
Dark blue	Madeira 9810/338 (3) with Madeira 9810/375 (3) (combine one thread of each)
Light blue	Madeira 9810/490 (2) Madeira 9810/333 (2) (combine one thread of each)
Dark gray	Appleton's crewel yarn 998 (1 hank or 4 skeins) or Paterna 221
Gold	Madeira Glissen Gloss gold braid 02 (1)

Quantities are shown in parentheses.

Golden Bough Brooch

This design is a detail from the Golden Bough, a woven silk and linen textile designed by Morris or Dearle. It has an elegance that reminds me of Art Nouveau. One of the original color combinations has a matte linen background with the contrasting shimmer of gold and olive green silk for the flowers and leaves. I thought that color combination went particularly well with the old gold of the brooch, which is in a style that recalls the heavy gold settings the Victorians liked to use for cameos and similar pieces.

DESIGN SIZE: $1^1/3$ x 1in (3.5 x 2.5cm) approx.
STITCH COUNT: 39 x 27

MATERIALS
Piece of 30-count silk gauze
Madeira No. 40 metallic threads as listed
in the key on page 42
Size 26 tapestry needle
$1^1/2$ x $1^1/4$ in (4 x 3cm) old gold brooch

1. Silk gauze is easy to work. It is like interlock canvas in construction but is quite transparent, so tidy fastening off is necessary. Mark the central guidelines just as you would if you were working on a larger scale (see page 118).
2. It is usually best to work with a frame. Some very small pieces can be mounted on a square of cardboard with the middle cut out. Attach the gauze with sticky tape, glue or staples round the edge.
3. Work the embroidery, using a single strand over one thread of the gauze. Embroider with cross stitch, taking care not to carry lengths of thread over empty spaces. The flowers are out-

lined in backstitch with the antique gold thread specified on page 42.

4. The brooch has a fastening which can swing around to allow you to wear the brooch vertically or horizontally. Adjust it for a tall oval. Remove the guidelines, press gently with a dry iron if necessary (see page 119), and cut out the gauze using the template in the brooch pack. If this template is a pale color and it will make a good background for the embroidery. Finally, assemble the brooch according to the manufacturer's instructions.

Flower Pendant

This design is based on a very typical Morris flower from a late wallpaper called Flora. In his design the flower is shown in yellow and cream, but I did not feel these colors would show up well enough in this sort of scale. So I have chosen stronger hues of blue and tan instead, which Morris favored in the pieces he designed for embroidery.

DESIGN SIZE: 1^1/₃in (3.5cm) diameter approx.
STITCH COUNT: 39 x 39

MATERIALS
Small piece of 30-count silk gauze
Stranded cottons as listed in the
key on page 42
Size 26 tapestry needle
1^5/₈-in-diameter (4.1cm) round gilt pendant

1. Follow steps 1 and 2 of the Golden Bough Brooch.
2. This brooch is worked in half cross stitch, using a single strand of floss over one thread of the gauze. It is easiest to work the dark blue background first then fill in. Be careful not to take the floss across areas that are going to be left blank.
3. Press gently with a cool iron if necessary (see page 119). Remove the guidelines and cut out carefully, using the pendant template or acetate as a guide. Mount according to the manufacturer's instructions, using the cream card behind the gauze.

A selection of the jewels from this Medieval collection (opposite, from top to bottom): Golden Bough Brooch, Silver Leaves Brooch and Flower Pendant. The St. James Carnation Pendant is shown on page 42.

Silver Leaves Brooch

This is another brooch with an antique look. I wanted to do a design with leaves only, because to William Morris, leaves were the basic element that he used to structure his designs. The ones in this brooch are based on the background of his Chrysanthemum design, where they are used in a light gold on a dark background. I have chosen to work them in silver on black to complement the frame.

DESIGN SIZE: ^{3}/₄ x 1in (2 x 2.5cm) approx.
STITCH COUNT: 24 x 30

MATERIALS
Small piece of 28-count Zweigart
evenweave Quaker Cloth in black
Madeira No 40 metallic thread in silver
Scrap of black iron-on interfacing
Size 26 tapestry needle
1^1/₂- x 1^1/₄-in (4 x 3cm) silver twisted brooch

1. This piece should be worked on a frame. Mark the central horizontal and vertical guidelines with basting (see page 118).
2. To make this design, use a single strand of silver over one thread of the fabric. It is worked in petit point (see page 120).
3. When you have embroidered the design, remove the guidelines and press. I usually bond these small pieces to iron-on interfacing before cutting them out.
4. The brooch can be worn vertically or horizontally, depending on which way you prefer to arrange the fastener. It's a good idea to adjust it for a tall oval. Cut out the fabric, using the template in the pack. Assemble the brooch according to the manufacturer's instructions.

St. James Carnation Pendant

This pendant uses a carnation from the St. James silk damask, produced when Morris and Co was commissioned to redecorate parts of St. James's Palace in London. The damask design is basically a diamond-shaped network of leaves with the spaces filled with roses, carnations, and bellflowers, and has a two-tone effect — light rose pink on dark, or dark on light. It was also produced in gold and other color combinations including blue.

DESIGN SIZE: ³/₄ x 1¹/₄ in (2 x 3cm) approx.
STITCH COUNT: 23 x 33

MATERIALS
Small piece of 28-count Jobelan evenweave in rose pink (NJ29.62)
Small piece iron-on interfacing
Stranded cotton as listed in the key on this page
Size 26 tapestry needle
1⁷/₈-x 1¹/₂-in gilt pendant (48 x 40mm) with 24in (61cm) chain

1. This piece should be worked on a frame. Mark the central horizontal and vertical guidelines with tacking (see page 118).
2. The design is worked using a single strand of floss over one thread of the fabric. It is worked in petit point (see page 120).
3. After you have embroidered the design, remove the guidelines and press (see page 119). I suggest bonding these small pieces to iron-on Vilene before cutting them out. Be careful to position the carnation carefully before you cut.
4. Assemble in the frame according to the manufacturer's instructions.

St. James Pendant

GOLDEN BOUGH BROOCH KEY

Colour	Thread
	Madeira Metallic No. 40
Gold	Gold-6
Antique gold	251
Backstitch in Antique gold	

FLOWER PENDANT KEY

Color	DMC	Anchor	Madeira
Dark blue	930	1035	1712
Medium blue	932	1033	1710
Light blue	3753	1031	1708
Cream	Ecru	387	Ecru
Tan	402	1047	2307

SILVER LEAVES BROOCH KEY

Color	Thread
	Madeira Metallic No. 40
Silver	Silver

ST. JAMES CARNATION PENDANT KEY

Color	DMC	Anchor	Madeira
Dark pink	3685	1028	0602

You will need only a little of each color. One spool or skein of each will leave plenty to spare.

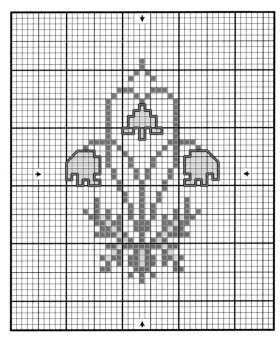

GOLDEN BOUGH BROOCH

MADIERA

Gold-6   251

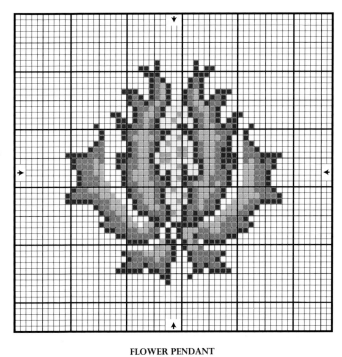

FLOWER PENDANT

DMC

930   932   3753   Ecru   402

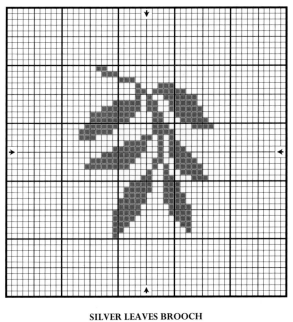

SILVER LEAVES BROOCH

MADIERA

Silver

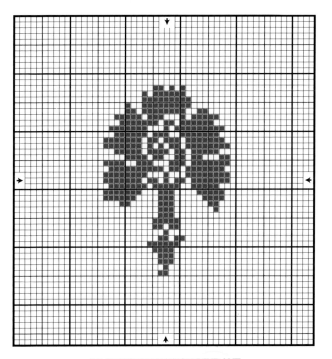

ST. JAMES CARNATION PENDANT

DMC

3685

Evenlode Tray and Coasters

This tray is an adaptation of Morris's Evenlode chintz, one of many designs he produced with a very dark blue-green background. The flowers, leaves, and stems in clear reds, yellows, blues, and greens that he placed against that background are thus clearly delineated. Such a strong design would be a little overpowering in the small area of a coaster, so here I have used only a detail from the flower at the center of the tray design to produce a motif that links the tray and coasters.

In Morris's original, the whole surface is decorated with meandering and coiling stems of foliage and flowers, studded at regular intervals with large, dominating pink and white motifs with an oriental appearance. I have chosen this particular flower as the centerpiece of the tray embroidery, depicting it, as Morris did, in cross section, showing the seed case. This seed-case design struck me as being just right for the coasters, with its strong yet simple forms.

To create an oval design that would not look too fussy for a tray, I have had to omit some of the other flowers that Morris used and to tame the profusion of twining forms growing from the continuous branches that figured in the original chintz. However, the S-bend motif that underlies his design has been re-created in my adaptation.

Morris loved to base his designs on traditional textile forms, and this one captures the fusion of English and Indian motifs that has been a characteristic of textiles in Britain since the 17th century, when crewel-work embroidery imitated the newly imported textiles from the Orient.

Evenlode Tray

Finished size: 9 x 12in (23 x 30cm)
Stitch count: 144 x 184

MATERIALS

13 x 16in (33 x 41cm) 18-count Aida in navy
Stranded floss as listed in the
key on page 49
Size 26 tapestry needle
Wooden serving tray measuring
12 x 16in (30 x 41cm) with oval insert

1. Mark the central horizontal and vertical guidelines with basting (see page 118). Because this is a finely detailed design, I recommend working extra guidelines, preferably in another color, 40 squares to left and right, above and below the center lines.

2. The design is embroidered with two strands of floss over one block of the fabric. Count carefully and keep checking your position against the guidelines as you work.

3. When you have finished, remove the guidelines and press (see page 119).

4. Assemble under the oval cutout and glass according to the maker's instructions.

Variations

1. The design has been worked on a very fine scale to fit the tray. It could be made much larger to use on a piano stool, for example, or a rectangular workbox or footstool.

If you use 14-count fabric, the size will be approximately 12 x 15in (30 x 38cm); on 11-count Aida or 20-count evenweave it will be about 15 x 19in (38 x 48cm). The navy color is available in all these counts of fabric.

The margin of fabric around the design could be enlarged to adapt it for larger items. Use the design to cover any rectangular or oval shape, or as pillows; it would also look very good on one of those long bags that embroiderers make to carry embroidery frames around.

2. Try the design on backgrounds of different colors. It could be adapted for a pale background, perhaps a traditional ecru, by simply adding a dark backstitched outline around the white petals.

Evenlode Coasters

The coasters use a detail from the elaborate central motif of the tray, which Morris seems to have based on the traditional pomegranate design. The shape suggests a tree bearing fruit, and its position inside a seed case suggests fertility and the continuous cycle of rebirth. In the tray design the tree shape is outlined by white stitches. Here it is embroidered in navy on a white background. It is a simple but attractive motif which could also be used for brooches or pendants on a higher-count fabric (see page 116), or for a greeting card.

DESIGN SIZE: to fit a 3¼in (8cm) circle
STITCH COUNT: 36 x 46

MATERIALS
7 x 7in (18 x 18cm) 18-count fine Aida in white for each coaster
4 x 4in (10 x 10cm) lightweight, white iron-on interfacing for each coaster
Stranded floss as listed in the key
Size 26 tapestry needle
Round acrylic coasters 3¼in (8cm) (see Suppliers, page 126)

1. Mark the central horizontal and vertical guidelines with basting (see page 118).
2. To embroider the design, use two strands of floss over one block of the fabric.
3. When you have finished, remove the guidelines and press (see page 119).
4. Iron on the interfacing, centering it in the middle of the design.
5. Use the template provided as a guide for cutting out the circle.
6. Assemble according to the manufacturer's instructions.

Variations

1. Choose a black fabric and work the tree in gold and the nuts, seeds and fruit in silver.
2. Mount the design in a metallic card or frame it.
3. You can produce the tree motif on a small scale for a pendant.

EVENLODE COASTER KEY

Color	DMC	Anchor	Madeira
Navy blue	336(1)	150(1)	1007(1)
Dark pink	815(1)	1005(1)	0513(1)

The coasters were stitched with DMC stranded floss. The alternatives may not be exact color equivalents. Quantities are shown in parentheses.

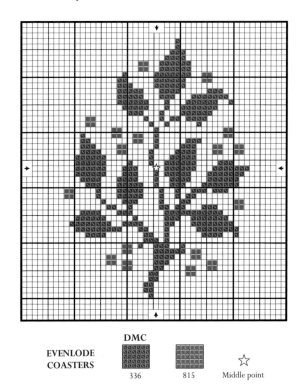

	DMC		
EVENLODE COASTERS	336	815	☆ Middle point

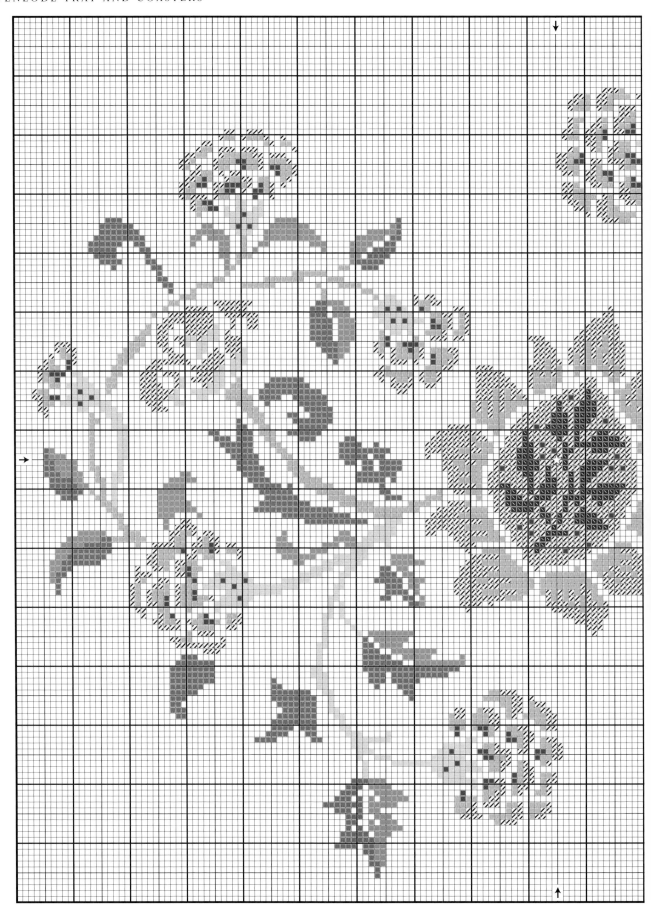

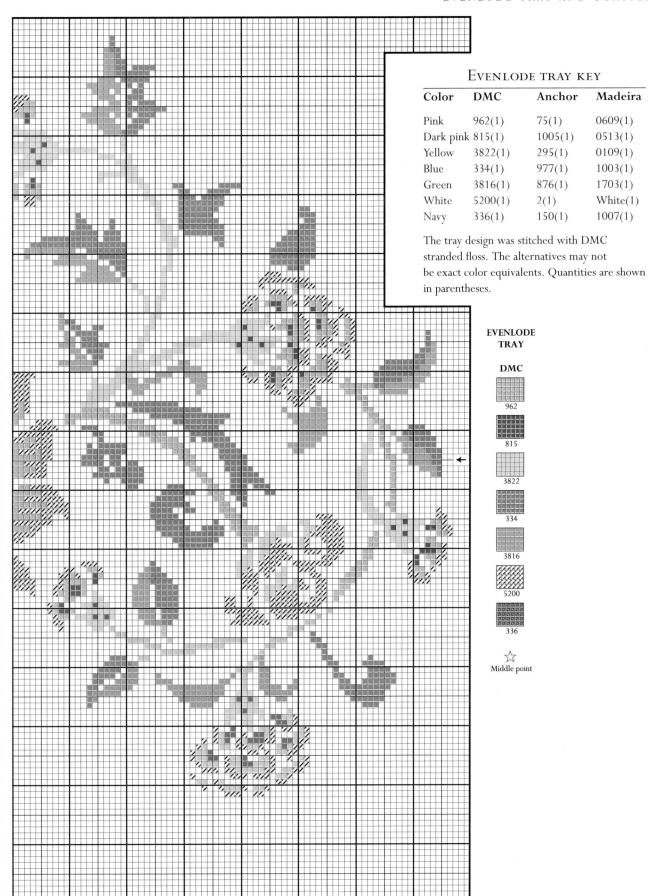

EVENLODE TRAY KEY

Color	DMC	Anchor	Madeira
Pink	962(1)	75(1)	0609(1)
Dark pink	815(1)	1005(1)	0513(1)
Yellow	3822(1)	295(1)	0109(1)
Blue	334(1)	977(1)	1003(1)
Green	3816(1)	876(1)	1703(1)
White	5200(1)	2(1)	White(1)
Navy	336(1)	150(1)	1007(1)

The tray design was stitched with DMC stranded floss. The alternatives may not be exact color equivalents. Quantities are shown in parentheses.

EVENLODE TRAY

DMC

962

815

3822

334

3816

5200

336

☆
Middle point

The Kelmscott Press Designs

All these designs were inspired by the beautiful handprinted books to which Morris devoted the last years of his life. He established the Kelmscott Press in 1890 with the intention of reviving the art of fine printing and bookmaking.

Morris's inspiration was his collection of medieval manuscripts and early printed books. When he was younger, he had produced hand-made books as presents, using calligraphy and painted decoration. And by doing so, he had already developed a highly decorative personal style. Since the Kelmscott Press books were to be printed, he had to limit himself almost entirely to black and white. But in his hands that does not seem a limitation. Each pair of pages was planned with such contrasts of elaborate pattern, illustration, plain text, capitals, and black on white and vice versa that the effect is of great richness and variety.

The Kelmscott Press designs (clockwise from top left): Grapevine Bookmark, Card, Photograph Frame, Leaves Bookmark, and Book Cover.

It is this contrast of dark on light and light on dark, combined with Morris's flowing foliage shapes, that distinguish these designs. The photograph frame is based on a border decoration in his *Works of Geoffrey Chaucer* and uses the flowing leaves and background stems of his design. However, while Morris used white on black for this design, I see this as a frame for a special photograph; and to emphasize its importance, I chose gold on black, which retains the light-on-dark balance of the original.

The two bookmark designs are based on pieces of border. The grapevine one was inspired by the design for the cover of *Works of Geoffrey Chaucer*, which was eventually executed in tooled leather. The vine is a most adaptable plant, eminently suited to pattern making, as medieval illuminators had discovered. Its contrast of large leaves, round grapes, sinuous stems, and tendrils was used again and again.

The embroidery of the other items is based on the decorative capital letters designed by Morris and shows a variety of effects with light and dark backgrounds. A complete charted alphabet can be found on pages 59 to 61.

The Paperweight.

Photograph Frame

This frame of stylized leaves has been designed to fit the most popular print size, but it can be worked on a larger count of fabric to accommodate the next larger size.

Finished size: 8- x 10-in (20 x 25cm), window to fit a 4- x 6-in (10 x 15cm) photo; or 9 x 11½in (23 x 29cm) to fit a 5- x 7-in (13 x 18cm) photo
Stitch count: 114 x 144

MATERIALS

12 x 14in (30 x 36cm) 16-count Aida in black; for the larger size, 13 x 16in (33 x 41cm) 14-count Aida in black
Alternatively, use 9- x 12- in (23 x 30cm) piece of 14-count Aida Plus (see Step 16)
5 spools Kreinik Very Fine Braid in gold
Size 24 tapestry needle
Medium-weight black iron-on interfacing, same size as Aida
Stiff cardboard (mat board) to stretch the embroidery over: 8 x 10in (20 x 25cm) for the smaller size, 9 x 11½in (23 x 29cm) for the larger
2-oz (50g) batting, minimum 8 x 10in (20 x 25cm) (optional)
8- x 10-in (20 x 25cm) or 9- x 11½-in (23 x 29cm) hardboard backing sheet with prop or stiff cardboard for back
Black fabric to cover the backing – minimum 9 x 21in (23 x 53cm) for the smaller size
Black sewing thread
Strong thread for lacing
2 small curtain rings and thin cord for a suspended frame
Craft knife
Pins
Tailor's chalk

PHOTOGRAPH FRAME ▦ Kreinik Very Fine Braid in gold ●—●—● Guide line ☆ Middle point

1. A frame is recommended for working this design, see page 117.

2. All the stitches are made in the same thread. The dotted line shown on the chart is just a guide to help you to position the border. Begin by marking the central horizontal and vertical guidelines with basting (see page 118). Then add the border guideline. Mark the top of the work.

3. The embroidery is done with one strand of Very Fine Braid. Do not continue with a length if it gets too frayed. I would suggest not using lengths of more than 20in (50cm).

4. Work the design, beginning at one of the guidelines. Keep checking your position.

5. When you have finished, remove the guidelines and press the work (see page 119). Bond the interfacing to the back, using a dry iron and medium heat.

6. Prepare the mat board. Cut it to 8 x 10in (20 x 25cm), or 9 x 11½ in (23 x 29cm) for the larger frame. Cut an opening from the center of the mat. This should be 5¾ x 3¾in (15 x 9.5cm) or, for the larger frame, 4¾ x 6¾in (12 x 17cm). If you are using batting, cut it to the same size as the mat. It will not give a very pronounced effect, but can help to disguise the odd wrinkle.

7. Assemble the layers — board, then batting, then embroidery. The embroidery needs to be right side up and placed centrally. Check this carefully with a ruler.

8. Put pins through the Aida into the edge of the board to hold it (Fig. 1). Verify that the design lines up straight around the opening, and that the grain of the fabric is straight.

9. Carefully turn the layers over. To be precise, you might want to mark around the edges and the opening — very close to the board — on the wrong side of the embroidery, using tailor's chalk. You can then remove the fabric from the board and stay-stitch around the inside edge

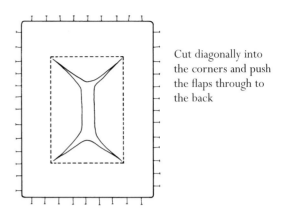

Fig. 1 Photograph frame from the front, showing the embroidered fabric pinned over the board.

with a small machine stitch and black thread to strengthen the corners. This is the a strandard approach to inside corners.

10. Reassemble the layers. With sharp scissors, carefully cut from the center into the corners of the opening (see Fig. 1). Push the flaps through and trim the excess fabric to 1in (2.5cm) all around.

11. Fold the fabric over the outside edges. Be certain that the work is still square.

12. Using buttonhole or linen thread, lace the Aida over the board, folding in the fabric to miter the corners as you go. Use a long length of thread, for ideally it should go all around. Begin by fastening securely with a knot, then double stitch and pull the thread tight as you lace (see Fig. 2). Make sure that the grain of the

Cut diagonally into the corners and push the flaps through to the back

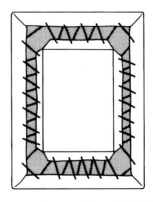

Fig. 2 Photograph frame from the back, showing lacing of the fabric over the board.

fabric on the front is kept straight. This is the correct way to do it. If your work is perfect and smooth, you can also glue the turned-over edges to the board. But with that method you will find it difficult to apply tension as evenly as you can with lacing.

13. Prepare the backing board. It should be exactly the same size as the front piece. If it is plain cardboard without a strut, just cut the backing fabric twice as big as the board plus seam allowances. Fold it over the board, turn in the edges, and sew around using ladder stitch (see page 121). If you have a board with a strut, take a slightly larger piece of fabric and fold it around the board so that the seam coincides with the hinge. Again, turn in the edges and stitch in place using ladder stitch, leaving a gap when you get to the hinge.

14. Place the two pieces wrong sides together. Ladder-stitch the two together, leaving a gap on one side so that you can put the photo in. This gap can be left for adjusting the photograph, or stitched up if you prefer.

15. If you wish to hang the photograph frame, attach two curtain rings to the backing fabric about a third of the way down from the top. Thread a cord through the rings to enable it to hang from a hook. An alternative finish would be to omit the backing board and use the front piece as a mat to fit within a frame, preferably without glass.

16. If you prefer, you can use Aida Plus instead of conventional Aida. Aida Plus is bonded and can be used without finishing the edges. It would be suitable if you wanted to use the embroidery as a mat inside a picture frame. In that case, the embroidery should be worked as above, though without using a frame. The opening and the outside measurements can be drawn on the back. To cut the opening using a sharp craft knife, run the blade along a metal straightedge. Assemble inside a picture frame.

Grapevine Bookmark

This design is a favorite of mine. I have translated the black and white of Morris's original drawing into black and gold on white. The Aida band I have chosen has a metallic gold edging which echoes the gold of the grapes. A gold tassel gives it a finishing touch.

FINISHED SIZE: 2 x 8 $\frac{1}{4}$in (5 x 21cm),
STITCH COUNT: 20 x 96

MATERIALS
10-in (25cm) length of 2-in (5cm) wide Aida
Band in white with gold edging
One skein black stranded floss
One pack Madeira Metallic No. 5
gold (5017)
Small piece of white medium-weight
iron-on interfacing
10-in (25cm) length of 1$\frac{1}{2}$-in (4cm) white
satin ribbon
Size 24 tapestry needle
White sewing thread

1. Mark the central horizontal and vertical guidelines on the Aida band with basting (see page 118).

2. For the black embroidery, use two strands. Do not carry lengths of black floss over blank areas on the back as it will show through to front.

3. The gold is worked with Madeira Metallic No. 5. Use it as it comes — four strands twisted loosely together.

4. When you have finished, remove the guidelines and press with a dry iron at medium heat (see page 119).

5. Cut a piece of interfacing measuring 1$\frac{1}{2}$ x 8$\frac{1}{4}$in (4 x 21cm). Fold it in half lengthwise to find the center and cut the last 1in (2.5cm) diagonally to form a point. Arrange it on the back of the embroidery, with the pointed part just below the bottom of the embroidery (see photograph on pages 50 and 51). Make sure that the amount left on each side is equal. Iron onto the Aida band.

6. Place the right side of the ribbon facing the right side of the embroidery. It will not be quite as wide as the Aida band. Pin it to hold it in place, then turn over and stitch the pieces together along the pointed edge of the interfacing (see Fig. 3). Trim away excess fabric and turn the point. Press it. Now slip stitch the ribbon invisibly to the

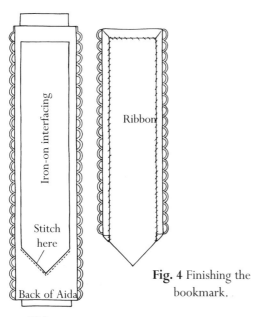

Fig. 3 Adding the interface.

Fig. 4 Finishing the bookmark.

back of the band; turning the band over at a length of approx 8¼in (21cm) and trim the hem to about ½in (1cm). Turn the corners in neatly and slip stitch the turned-in edge of the ribbon over it to finish (see Fig. 4).

7. Make a tassel from the gold thread (see Fig. 5). Cut a piece of cardboard 2¾in (7cm) long and wind the gold thread around it five or six times. Thread a needle with another length of the gold thread and run it underneath the

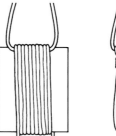

Fig. 5 Making the tassel

strands at the top of the card. Knot the ends loosely for now. (You will use them to sew it on.) Find a helper to slip the cardboard out and hold the threads while you bind another length of gold around at the top. Knot it firmly, then thread the ends down through the binding and trim them to the length of the tassel. Cut the looped ends. Now unknot the ends and sew the tassel neatly to the bottom of the bookmark.

Leaves Bookmark

This design, based on one of the Kelmscott Press borders, shows two of Morris's favorite acanthus leaves with a stylized flower between them. Avoiding bulk is always important when making bookmarks, so I chose to work this one on perforated paper. This was available to Victorian embroiderers and has recently been reintroduced. One of its advantages is that it does not need any hems, and the finishing stage is merely a matter of gluing another piece of the paper to the back.

FINISHED SIZE: 2 x 8in (5 x 20cm)
STITCH COUNT: 18 x 85

MATERIALS
One sheet of silver perforated paper
(equivalent to 14-count)
One skein black stranded floss
Size 22 tapestry needle
Paper glue
12in (30cm) very narrow silver ribbon

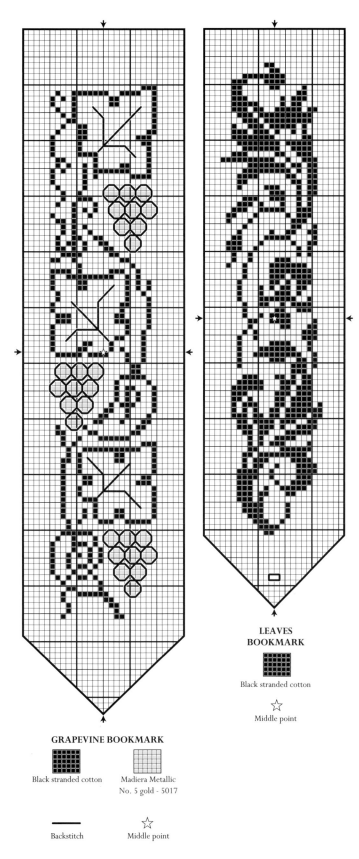

1. The sheet of paper will be enough for several other projects as well as the bookmark. Leave one or two holes outside the edge lines when you cut it out in case the edges get grubby.

2. Use three strands of floss at a time because the holes are larger than in fabric. Work the embroidery using a stab stitch method — back to front, front to back. Do not bend the paper and try not to carry the thread across empty areas.

3. Next, cut the paper to the size shown on the chart. Cut down a row of holes, close to the solid part. The edges will be slightly lumpy, but should not have snags which can catch on things. Cut another piece the same size.

4. Place the pieces with wrong sides together, lining up the holes so that it looks like one neat piece. When it is right, glue around the inside edges with paper glue or rubber cement, and press the pieces firmly together until they stick together securely.

5. Use a sharp pair of pointed scissors to cut out the hole for the ribbon (see chart). Double the ribbon, thread the loop through the hole, and pull the ends through the loop. Trim the ends on the diagonal.

LEAVES BOOKMARK

Black stranded cotton

☆
Middle point

GRAPEVINE BOOKMARK

Black stranded cotton   Madiera Metallic
No. 5 gold - 5017

——— Backstitch   ☆ Middle point

Detail of the Leaves Bookmark.

Book Cover

This simple design incorporates one of the leaf-decorated initials that Morris created for the Kelmscott Press. Choose your own initial, or an A for addresses, a B for birthdays, and so on. The cover is worked in silver on black, but you could use any strongly contrasting combination that appeals to you.

FINISHED SIZE: to cover notebook about
4¹/₄ x 6in (11 x 15cm)
STITCH COUNT: 49 x 71

MATERIALS
Hardback notebook from a
stationery store
8 x 18in (20 x 46cm) 14-count Aida in black
8 x 18in (20 x 46cm) black lining material
6 x 9in (15 x 23cm) black medium-weight
iron-on interfacing
Kreinik Very Fine Braid 001 in silver
(2 spools)
Black sewing thread

1. Fold the Aida in half with the short sides together. Measure ¹/₂in (1cm) from the fold and baste a guideline to mark the left edge of the front cover (see Fig. 5). Mark the lines around the other edges with basting (measure your

cover), then mark the central horizontal and vertical guidelines on your rectangle (see page 118).
2. All the initials are the same size, so choose whichever you like from the charts on pages 59–61.
3. The embroidery is worked using one strand of Very Fine Braid.
4. When you have finished, press the embroidery, but do not remove the edge guidelines.
5. Turn to page 124 for instructions on making a book cover.

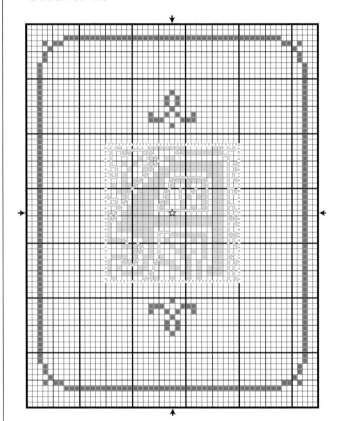

BOOK COVER

▦ Kreinik Very Fine Braid in silver	·········· Edge of space for initial	☆ Middle point

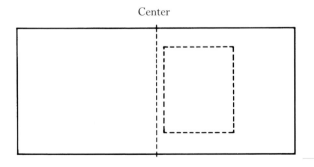

Center

Fig. 5 Book cover showing placement of embroidery

Card and Paperweight

These designs show two of the numerous ways to use the initials charted on pages 59–61. Use the initials wherever you want to personalize special items. The letters themselves have a chunky, primitive, handcut look, designed by Morris in the style of the early books he so admired. Each is set in a foliage decoration to make a square block. Photographs of the card and paperweight can be seen on pages 50–52.

DESIGN SIZE: about 2¼in (6cm) on 11-count fabric or 22-count, worked over two threads; about 1¾in (4.5cm) on 14 -count fabric or 28-count, worked over two threads; about 1½in (4cm) on 16-count fabric or 32-count, worked over two threads; about 1½in (4cm) on 18-count fabric or 36-count, worked over two threads
INITIAL STITCH COUNT: 25 x 25

PAPERWEIGHT
MATERIALS
Small piece of 32-count evenweave Belfast linen in white
Black stranded floss
White iron-on interfacing
Size 26 tapestry needle
2-in square (5cm) glass paperweight kit

1. Work the design using two strands over two threads.
2. Bond the interfacing to the back and cut out, using the template provided by the paperweight manufacturer. Assemble according to the instructions.

CARD
MATERIALS
4 x 6in (10 x 15cm) 28-count evenweave fabric (The example was worked on Jobelan in antique white.)
Black stranded floss
White iron-on interfacing
Size 24 tapestry needle
Three-fold card medium size with 3¼in (8cm) diameter circular opening

1. Work the chosen initial using two strands of floss over two threads.
2. Bond the interfacing to the back and mount it in the card.

KELMSCOTT ALPHABET    Cross stitch — Backstitch

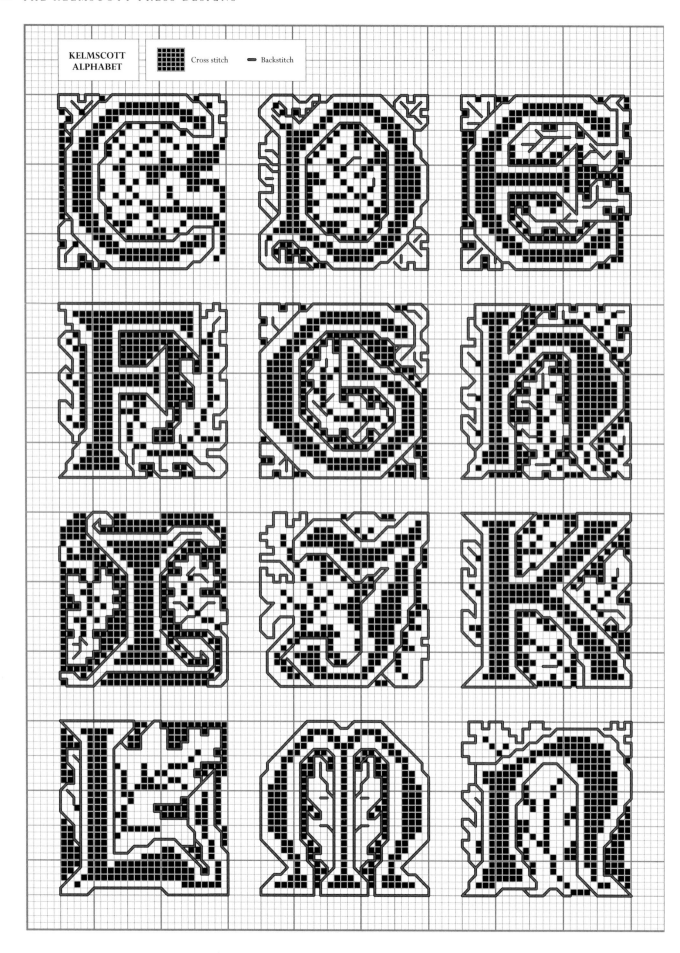

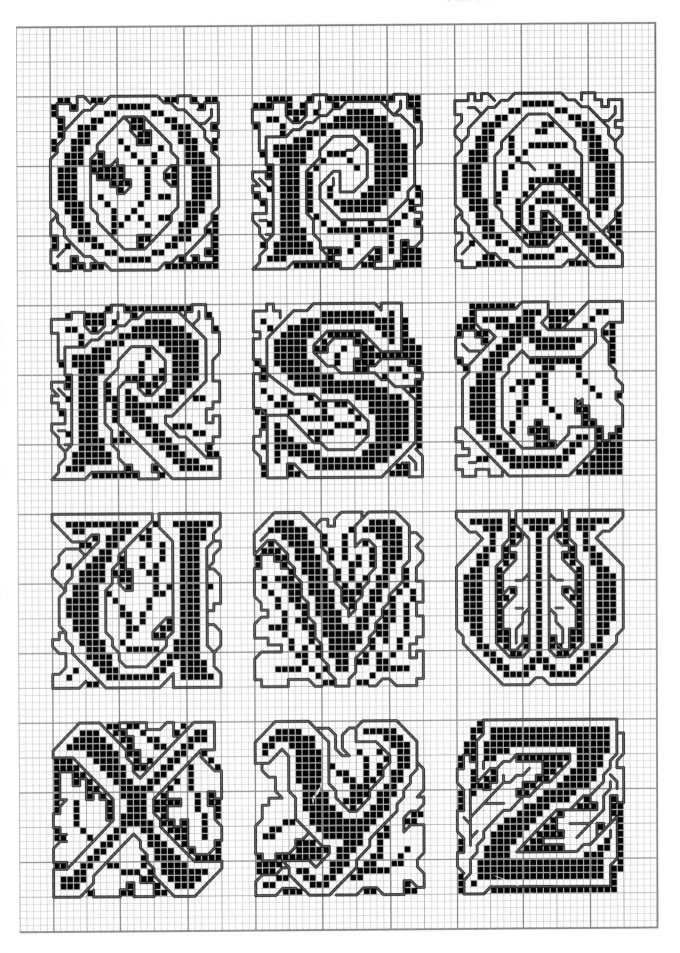

The Pimpernel Footstool

An embroidered footstool adds a charmingly period touch to a room and also provides a practical way to rest tired or achy feet. and Morris's Pimpernel design struck me as ideal for adapting to this use. To complement the style, I chose a footstool in dark mahogany with small, rounded feet.

In the Pimpernel design, from the 1870s, Morris trained his stems and leaves into regimented spirals, rather more reminiscent of wrought iron than foliage. It is one of his vertical "turn over" designs, in which mirror image pairs of motifs are formed. The wallpaper is made up of pairs of the motif used in the footstool, alternating above and below with similar motifs in which the large flower faces the other way.

I have allowed the rim of wood to take the place of the circling brown stem in the original. Used in this way, the long, straplike leaves seem to grow up from underneath the footstool, framing the pimpernels, which make a bright circlet of flowers around the splendid central gray-green poppy.

FINISHED SIZE: 12in (30cm) in diameter
STITCH COUNT: 200 x 200

MATERIALS
20 x 20in (50 x 50cm) 16-count
Zweigart Aida in bay leaf green
Stranded floss as listed in the
key on page 65
Size 26 tapestry needle
12in (30cm) diameter footstool
Strong thread and needle

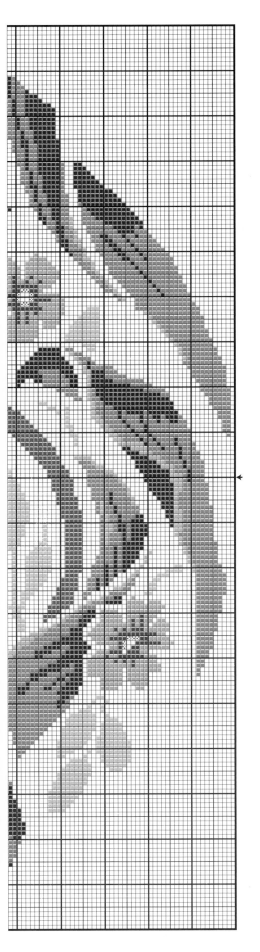

**PIMPERNEL
FOOTSTOOL**

DMC

500

3817

3756

928

924

3768

926

564

517

813

3772

☆
Middle point

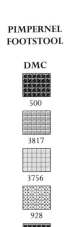

1. Mark the central horizontal and vertical guidelines with basting (see page 118).

2. This is a complex design, so I recommend marking extra guidelines (using a different-colored thread) at 20, 40, and 60 squares on each side of the center lines.

3. It will probably help if you make a color palette from a piece of cardboard with holes punched along the sides. Knot a short piece of floss through the holes. Arrange the colors in groups — poppy, pimpernels, long leaves — and write in the numbers next to the color.

4. Work the design using two strands of floss over one block of the fabric. Begin in the center and use the dark green first, because that color is used to outline the petals.

5. Fill in the poppy, then move out to the pimpernels. Finally, work the long leaves.

6. Leave the center guidelines for now, but remove the other guidelines and press carefully (see page 119).

7. Find the center of the footstool pad and place your embroidery over the pad, matching centers. (For cross stitch, a close-fitting pad is best; if yours is loose, you might wish to add a layer of batting and a covering piece of fabric to prevent the fibers from poking through.)

PIMPERNEL FOOTSTOOL KEY

Color	DMC	Anchor	Madeira
Dark green	500 (2)	683 (2)	1705 (2)
Peppermint	3817 (2)	875 (2)	1701 (2)
Silver	928 (2)	274 (2)	1709 (2)
Off-white	3756 (1)	1037 (1)	1001 (1)
Brown	3772 (1)	1007 (1)	2310 (1)
Blue	517 (1)	162 (1)	0911 (1)
Pale blue	813 (1)	161 (1)	0910 (1)
Leaf green	564 (2)	219 (2)	1208 (2)
Blue-green	3768 (3)	779 (3)	1707 (3)
Dark blue-green	924 (2)	851 (2)	1706 (2)
Light blue-green	926 (1)	850 (1)	1708 (1)

The footstool design was stitched using DMC floss. The alternative colors may not be exact color equivalents. Quantities are shown in parentheses.

8. Turn the stool over carefully and smooth the fabric out. You need to trim it so that there is a generous border of fabric — about 3in (8cm) in from the rim. You will turn your square of fabric into a circle.

9. Remove the fabric from the pad and run a gathering stitch all around about ³⁄₄in (2 cm) in from the edge, using a strong thread. I worked another row closer to the edge of the pad (see Fig. 1).

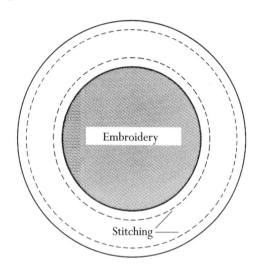

Fig. 1 Shaping the fabric to cover the pad

10. Put the fabric back on the pad and put a pin through the center to hold it in position. Smooth it out and hold it in place by pinning into the pad all around the edge. Turn it over and gather up the fabric at the back. Fasten the threads off securely. It might be necessary to press the fabric with a steam iron (use a cloth as well) to remove wrinkles. Lacing the fabric across from side to side can help to even it out.

11. When you are satisfied, fasten the fabric to the backing with a staple gun or upholstery tacks. Remove the pin and guidelines.

12. Assemble the stool according to the manufacturer's instructions.

Variations

1. To make a larger footstool, choose a 14-in (36cm) stool, and 28-count evenweave fabric, to be worked over two threads to give the equivalent of 14-count fabric. This color is available in Brittney and Quaker cloth but not in 14-count Aida.

2. Instead of making a footstool, you might prefer to use the design for a round pillow. Add a bold cord or a fringe edging.

3. I do not think that these colors would work on a background of a different color, but you could devise another color scheme entirely. This one is predominantly blue-green, but has a small area of contrast in the rust brown of the stem. This contrast is worth re-creating in whatever color scheme you choose.

4. The poppy is a sufficiently strong and attractive design to be used by itself without the pimpernels.

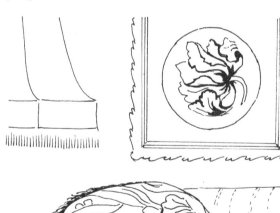

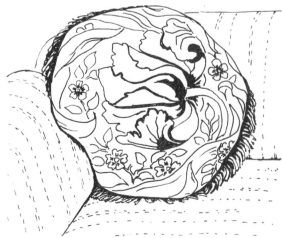

Pomegranate Bowl Lids

These two designs are based on the simpler motifs in the Pomegranate Chintz, which William Morris designed in the 1870s. I thought the colors were particularly attractive and very typical of Morris's palette, and the turned elm bowls for which the lids are designed are a per-fect foil for them. These bowls would make a suitable present for a man, providing ideal containers for cuff-links and other personal items.

The Pomegranate is one of a group of designs that show a strong similarity to the Indian designs that were popular throughout the 19th century. It was produced at a time when Morris was working closely with Thomas Wardle, a dyer and printer who specialized in working with silk. Wardle imported his silk and some printed fabrics from India, so Morris would have been surrounded by the Oriental influence. He spent much time in Wardle's factory because the two men were collaborating in dyeing experiments, trying to relearn traditional

techniques. Meanwhile, Morris chose the best of the dyes that were then available, and the Pomegranate Chintz was one of the fabrics Wardle printed for Morris's company.

The motif of the pomegranate was one that Morris used often. An early wallpaper shows a quite natural version of it, but more often it is used in a very stylized form, often combined, as it is in the Pomegranate Chintz, with that other most decorative plant, the artichoke. He sometimes used cross sections through plant forms to produce a symmetrical and decorative effect. The many-layered fruit surrounded by leaves became a standard decorative motif, used on papers, fabrics, and frequently on carpets.

FINISHED SIZE: about 3in (8cm)
STITCH COUNT:
64 x 63 for Design 1,
58 x 59 for Design 2

MATERIALS
Two 6- x 6-in (15 x 15 cm) pieces of 22-count
Hardanger fabric in ecru
Stranded floss as listed in the key
Size 26 tapestry needle
Two wooden bowls with 3½-in diameter
(9cm) lids

1. Mark the central horizontal and vertical guidelines on the Hardanger fabric with basting (see page 118).
2. Embroider the design as indicated in the chart opposite. Use a single strand of floss over one double thread.
3. When you have finished, remove the guidelines and press (see page 119). Assemble the bowl lids according to the manufacturer's instructions.

Variations

These designs could be used for little framed pictures, or you could change the scale dramatically and work two pillows, perhaps to go with cane furniture. You can buy ecru-colored Aida in both 6- and 8-count. This would give a motif size of about 10in (25cm) on the 6-count fabric about 7½in (19cm) on the 8-count.

Add some space and a border in cross stitch or braid to complete the designs and make 16-in (41cm) pillows. Use the stranded floss undivided for working at this scale. As a rough guide, for the two designs (not including any kind of border), you will need about six skeins of the blue, four of the yellow, two of the red, and one of the brown.

POMEGRANATE BOWL KEY

Color	DMC	Anchor	Madeira
Yellow ocher	729(1)	890(1)	2212(1)
Indigo blue	930(1)	1035(1)	1712(1)
Rust red	3830(1)	5975(1)	0401(1)
Brown	632(1)	936(1)	2311(1)

The designs were stitched using DMC threads. The alternatives may not be exact color equivalents. Quantities are given in parentheses.

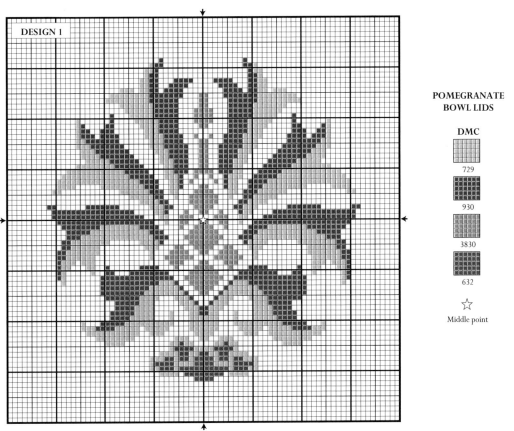

DESIGN 1

**POMEGRANATE
BOWL LIDS**

DMC

729

930

3830

632

☆
Middle point

DESIGN 2

Larkspur Tablecloth and Napkins

Morris's Larkspur wallpaper, on which these embroideries are based, is one of his most delicate and flowing designs, composed of curves and swirls of foliage in pastel colors on a white ground. Its white background and circles of flowers suggested to me its potential for a tablecloth decoration, accompanied by napkins with the same theme.

The Morris design is built on a parallel series of vertical stems that sway gently to right and left as they progress up the wall. They bear curving branches of peppermint green fern-like leaves entwined with the wreaths of flowers that inspired the embroidery designs. In the original, these motifs are composed of just three sprigs of flowers, the larkspur, the rose, and the little pink flowers, each with its distinctive leaf shape.

For the tablecloth design, I have repeated the sequence of flowers in order to create a larger circle with enough space in the center for a vase of flowers or a candlestick. The design is concentrated in the center of the cloth so that it can be displayed without being concealed by plates or dishes. A small sprig of each flower has been chosen for the napkins. The coloring of the flowers re-creates the look of the original, and I have used the predominant foliage color for the leaves in this adaptation.

Larkspur Tablecloth

This is a tablecloth for special occasions and is recommended for experienced embroiderers. It is big enough for an average table, which would seat six people comfortably. The fabric chosen is a traditional hard-wearing natural fabric — a half-cotton, half-linen evenweave blend called Quaker cloth.

FINISHED SIZE OF TABLECLOTH:
about 4½ x 8ft (1.3 x 2.4m)
STITCH COUNT: 200 x 200

MATERIALS
2¾yd (2.5m) 28-count Quaker cloth
(55in/140cm wide, 50% cotton/50% linen) in antique white. Alternatively, you could use100% cotton evenweave,
which has a linen look. This is available in the same width and color. If you need a wider cloth for your table, fabric which is 63in (160cm) wide, give a finished width of 5ft (1.5m).
Stranded floss as listed in the key on page 74
Size 24 tapestry needle

1. This is a large piece of fabric to manage, and some care is necessary in handling it. It is sensible to use a frame for this design. A 17-in (43cm) square plastic clip frame (see page 118) works fine. Keep the work wrapped in a sheet and lay the sheet out under the work while stitching to keep it off the floor.
2. Mark the central horizontal and vertical guidelines with basting (see page 118). I marked these on the chart with a yellow felt-tip pen and used a matching color for the guidelines. (The horizontal center line is at the bottom of the chart, which shows only half the design.) Because the center is empty and you need to know where to start, I recommend extra guide-lines at 50 and 100 stitches out in each direction. I marked the "50" lines in green and the "100s" in blue and matched the color of the lines on the chart and the stitched lines on the fabric (see Fig. 1). The marking takes time to do, but it is very reassuring as you work to know that the circle of flowers will join up. To count accurately, I counted two threads for each stitch and marked every 10 stitches with a pin. This way you can check your counting with some confidence. Extra care in counting at this stage can avoid unpicking later.
3. The chart shows half the design. Work the cloth with the top of the chart toward the selvage and the bottom of the chart along your center guideline. Then turn the chart upside down to work the bottom half.
4. The embroidery is worked with two strands of stranded floss over two threads of the fabric. When working the leaves, you can move from one to another without fastening off; thread the

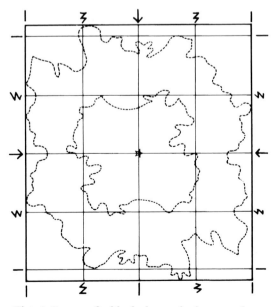

Fig. 1 Center of tablecloth, marked out ready to embroider.

floss through at the back until you reach a small gap. With the flowers, carry the floss from one petal to another on the same flower, but not from flower to flower. Take care whenever you are starting and finishing lengths of floss (see page 119) because the cloth is going to be washed frequently.

5. The order of working is up to you. Choose your favorite part first, but remember that it is sensible to start from an intersection of the guidelines. Keep checking your position against the guidelines as you proceed.

6. When you have completed the embroidery, work a narrow hem to finish the cloth, ideally using antique hemstitch (see page 121.)

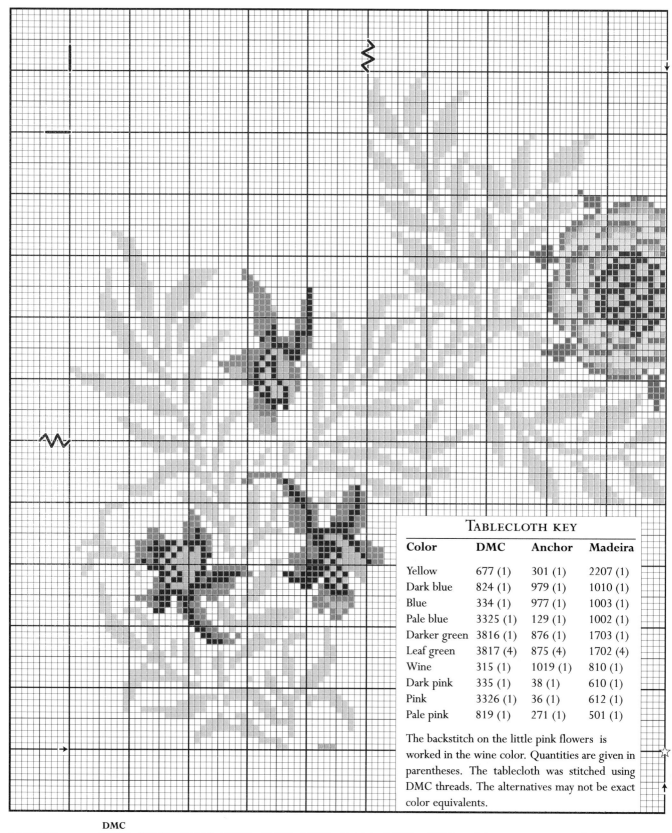

TABLECLOTH KEY

Color	DMC	Anchor	Madeira
Yellow	677 (1)	301 (1)	2207 (1)
Dark blue	824 (1)	979 (1)	1010 (1)
Blue	334 (1)	977 (1)	1003 (1)
Pale blue	3325 (1)	129 (1)	1002 (1)
Darker green	3816 (1)	876 (1)	1703 (1)
Leaf green	3817 (4)	875 (4)	1702 (4)
Wine	315 (1)	1019 (1)	810 (1)
Dark pink	335 (1)	38 (1)	610 (1)
Pink	3326 (1)	36 (1)	612 (1)
Pale pink	819 (1)	271 (1)	501 (1)

The backstitch on the little pink flowers is worked in the wine color. Quantities are given in parentheses. The tablecloth was stitched using DMC threads. The alternatives may not be exact color equivalents.

LARKSPUR TABLECLOTH

DMC

3816 3817 677 824 334 3325 315 335 3326 819 Backstitch 315 Positions for guidelines Middle point

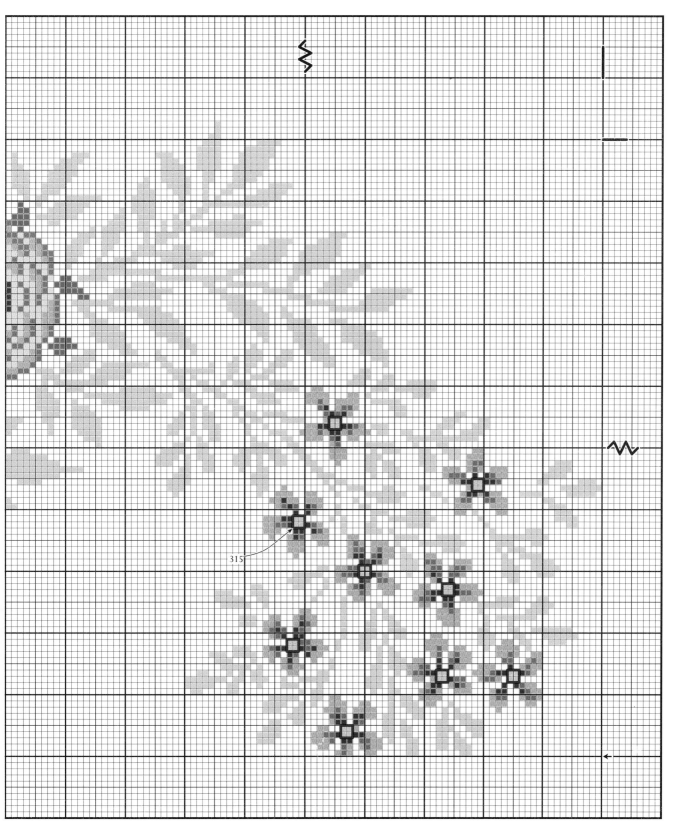

315

Rotate the pattern 180°
at the middle point to
complete the design

Larkspur Napkins

There are three designs for napkins — the blue larkspur, the pink rose, and the small pink flowers with the rounded leaves. They are based on the three flowers that form the floral wreaths on the Larkspur wallpaper. Each selection will make a motif to fit in a corner of a napkin. Make two of each design for a set of six, or choose your favorite motif and repeat it. If you like the tablecloth design but have not worked on evenweave before, try the napkins first.

FINISHED SIZE: 16¹/₂in (42cm) square
STITCH COUNT: 50 x 50

MATERIALS FOR SIX NAPKINS
1¹/₄yd (1m) 28-count Quaker cloth
55in-wide (wide), 50% cotton 50% linen)
in antique white.
Stranded floss as listed in the
key on page 79
Size 24 tapestry needle

1. Make each napkin 18¹/₂in (47cm) square (for maximum economy the size of the napkins has been chosen so that three can be cut from one width of 55in cloth).
2. To position your embroidery on the napkin, inspect each piece of fabric and decide which corner you want to decorate. The fabric has natural slubs, and some are quite noticeable. Choose the smoothest, most even corner, and mark it with a pin to remind you of your choice. Fold the fabric in half and then into quarters with your chosen corner on top.
3. Measure out from the folded sides and mark a position 5in (13cm) from the two folds (see Fig. 2). Where the lines meet is the place to center the embroidered motif. When you have

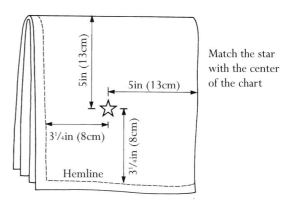

Match the star with the center of the chart

Fabric folded into quarters

Fig. 2 Napkin showing placement of embroidery.

worked the hem this point will be 3¹/₄in (8cm) from the oputer edges of the napkin, but the motif should be embroidered before the hem is made. It is helpful to baste guidelines, corresponding with the center lines indicated on the chart. The top right-hand corner of the chart should be closest to the center of the napkin.
4. Stitch the napkins according to the charts, using two strands of stranded floss over two threads of the fabric. A hoop large enough for the complete embroidery motif is strongly recommended.
5. These are items that will be washed frequently, so take care to start and finish lengths of floss securely (see page 119). Move from area to area by threading the floss through the backs of other stitches. Avoid carrying a thread over an empty area of fabric as it may show through.
6. When the embroideries are completed, a hem must be worked. Measure out from the guidelines another 3¹/₄in (8cm) and mark the line of the hem (see Fig. 2). The finished size should be 16¹/₂in (42cm) square, with a 1in (2.5cm) hem allowance. The fold for the hem should be straight along a thread of the fabric. A hand-worked hem (see page 121) would look special. But if time is limited, a neat job with the sewing machine is fine; use a thread that exactly matches the fabric. Neat corners are of

course essential no matter which method you choose. Follow the diagrams on page 123 to achieve a neat mitered effect.

Variations

The suggestions below assume that you will use the colors specified in the charts. However, William Morris wanted craftspeople to put something of themselves into everything they made. So in that spirit, please use the charts just as the starting point for creating something that is personal to you.

CLOTH FOR A SMALL ROUND TABLE

The tablecloth chart could be used to decorate a cloth to go over a little round occasional table. Choose a suitable fabric and embroider the pattern in the center of a 39-in (1m) square piece.

To mark a circle, begin by attaching a piece of string to a pin. With a cork mat underneath, put the pin in the center of the design. Measure 20in (50cm) along the string and tie a knot. Use this as a guide to mark out the edge of your circle. To finish the edge, turn over and press under a single hem. Finish the raw edge with a closely stitched wide zigzag stitch. Choose a deep lace edging of suitable color and weight to match fabric and pin the lace over the folded edge of the cloth. Stitch to attach the lace and finish the hem. Find a suitable undercloth in pale pink or blue to pick up the flower colors.

PILLOWS

The overall size of the wreath of flowers is 14in (36cm), when worked on 28-count evenweave or on 14-count Aida. You could make it bigger by choosing a 21-count evenweave or 11-count Aida, or smaller by choosing a fine linen or a 16- or 18-count Aida. Because the coloring is pale, it would show up well if you were to choose a very dark background color, which might be more practical for a throw pillow. Allow at least 2½in (6cm) around the edge of the embroidery to balance the space in the center. It could be made as a square or round pillow (see page 123).

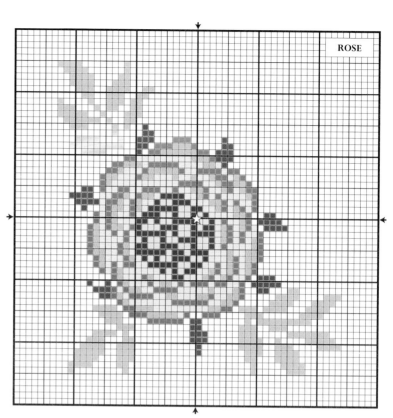

ROSE

GREETING CARD

The little flower design might be used to make a greeting card, perhaps with a pink or green card mount. To produce a medium size card choose a 16- or 18-count of Aida, an evenweave equivalent.

TRAY CLOTH

If you hold a mirror against the right-hand (stem) side of the Larkspur chart, you will see that it makes a pretty border design, which could be used at either end of a tray cloth to go with your tablecloth and napkins. It could also decorate table mats or make a border on a tea cozy, and it is delicate enough to be used to decorate dresser cloths. Remember that if you want to make it larger, you can choose a coarser (lower) count of fabric.

SMALL BAG OR PURSE

The rose chart could be used on the flap of a small purse, perhaps on a dramatic navy or

black fabric. If you make the purse with a strong piece of fabric, the rose embroidery could be applied to the flap. The edges and seam could be finished with a pink or green braid to match the embroidery. The same braid could make a shoulder strap.

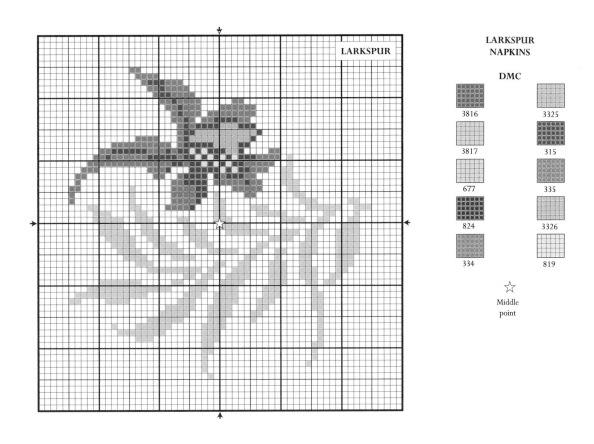

LARKSPUR

LARKSPUR NAPKINS

DMC

3816	3325
3817	315
677	335
824	3326
334	819

☆
Middle point

Napkin key

Color	DMC	Anchor	Madeira
Yellow	677 (1)	301(1)	2207(1)
Dark blue	824(1)	979(1)	1010(1)
Blue	334(1)	977(1)	1003(1)
Pale blue	3325(1)	129(1)	1002(1)
Darker green	3816(1)	876(1)	1703(1)
Leaf green	3817(2)	875(2)	1702(2)
Wine	315(1)	1019(1)	810(1)
Dark pink	335(1)	38(1)	610(1)
Pink	3326(1)	36(1)	612(1)
Pale pink	819(1)	271(1)	501(1)

The backstitch on the little pink flower chart was made in the wine color. The napkins were stitched using DMC threads. The alternatives may not be exact color equivalents. Quantities (given in parentheses) are enough for two of each design. Where one skein is shown, you will probably not need to buy any extra if you are making the tablecloth as well.

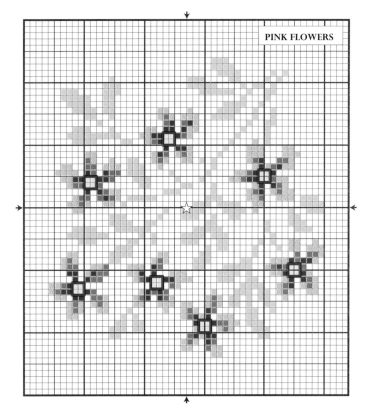

PINK FLOWERS

Wild Tulip Tea Party

The wild tulip used to grow in the meadows around Oxford, and Morris may have seen them there, or perhaps he copied them from his beloved Persian art. He preferred wildflowers to cultivated ones in most cases, admiring their simple shapes and gentle coloring.

The tea cozy can easily be adapted for a coffee pot simply by working it on a vertical rectangle of fabric.

The Wild Tulip wallpaper was one of Morris's popular monochrome designs. It uses two tones of pink as a background for white flowers, which are emphasized by a dark outline and which I have interpreted in backstitch.

In this design Morris used the darker pink in solid areas to show the form of flowers and leaves, as a stipple of dots for shading, and to give a lively texture to the background.

Structurally, this design has his familiar meandering stems climbing at a slight diagonal, a form he used again and again. Its inspiration was an early Italian textile at the South Kensington Museum (now the Victoria & Albert Museum), where he was an adviser on textiles, particularly renowned for his expertise on oriental carpets. Between the diagonal stems is a profusion of scattered tulips that mainly follow the direction of the stems, but some curl around in a contrary direction.

I have selected just three sprigs, which are used together in the tea cozy. I have moved one sprig down to complete a circle, emphasized by the stipple of spots. The place mats use just two of the flowers to decorate opposite diagonal corners.

Tea Cozy

FINISHED SIZE: 14 x 11in (36 x 28cm)
STITCH COUNT: 104 x 104

MATERIALS
Two 18- x 17-in (46 x 43cm) pieces
of 28-count evenweave Jobelan in
deep rose
Two 18- x 17-in (46 x 43cm) pieces of
firm white iron-on interfacing
Two 15½-in 12-in (39 x 30cm) pieces
of 8oz (225g) batting
Two 15½ x 12in (39 x 30cm) pieces
of lining fabric
Stranded floss as listed in the key
Size 24 tapestry needle
Matching sewing thread
1 yd (91cm) of twisted cord to finish

1. This fabric should be worked in a frame large enough to hold the entire design area (see page 118). If you use a hoop, it may be difficult to get rid of the marks. Begin by overcasting the edges, by hand or machine, to prevent fraying.
2. Mark the central horizontal and vertical guidelines with basting (see page 118).
3. Begin by working the cross stitch areas. The embroidery is stitched with two strands of stranded floss over two threads of fabric.
4. Next, work the backstitch, and again be sure to use two strands.
5. It does not matter if the spots are not positioned exactly where I have marked them; if you lose your place, just improvise. If necessary, cut a 7½-in-diameter (19cm) circle from a piece of ordinary writing or photocopy paper and pin it on, centered on the center lines, as a guide to where to stop the circle of spots.

6. To make the tea cozy, remove the guidelines and press (see page 119). Iron the interfacing on the front and back pieces.
7. Make a paper pattern. If you have a tea cozy, use it as a guide; otherwise, draw a rectangle 14 x 13in (36 x 33cm). Fold over a 2-in (5cm) hem along the bottom. Fold in half both ways to find the center. Draw curves in place of the top corners (see Fig. 1).

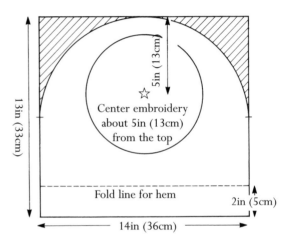

Fig. 1 Tea cozy pattern diagram.

8. The embroidery is centered very slightly above the middle of the tea cozy. Position it so that its center is 5in (13cm) down from the top. When you are happy with it, cut out the embroidered fabric, leaving a very generous seam allowance for minor adjustments when you fit it to the teapot. Cut another piece for the back from the spare fabric.
9. Assemble one piece of batting, the back, the front with right side facing the back, and the second piece of batting. Pin around the stitching line with long pins, and adjust the shape and size if necessary. I put a plastic bag around the teapot before I tried my cozy for fit, just in case drips might touch the embroidered side.
10. Stitch around the seam. Trim the edges, then turn up the hem. I found I had to curve mine slightly to make a good fit.

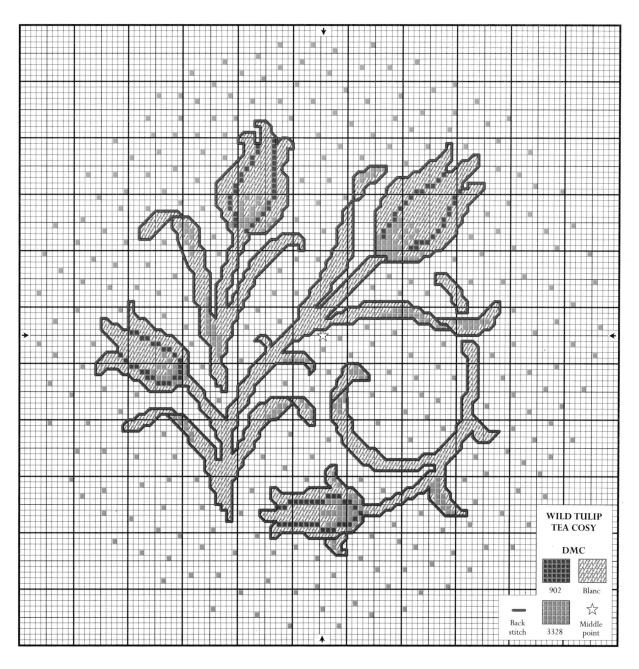

**WILD TULIP
TEA COSY**

DMC

902   Blanc

Back   3328   Middle
stitch   point

11. Make a lining to fit. The original template, with the hem cut off, can be used again. Slip stitch the lining in place, catching it to the inside of the seam. Turn up the bottom and stitch so that it covers the edge of the hem.

12. Fold the cord in two and make a loop in the top. Secure it with a few stitches. Slip stitch the cord around the cozy, concealing the seam. Tuck the ends inside and hide the ends in the seam of the lining.

WILD TULIP KEY

Color	DMC	Anchor	Madeira
Dark red	902(1)	897(1)	0601(1)
Pink	3328(1)	1024(1)	0406(1)
White	White(2)	2(2)	White(2)
Backstitch in Dark red			

The designs were stitched using DMC thread. The alternatives may not be exact color equivalents. Quantities sufficient for one tea cozy and two place mats are shown in parentheses.

83

The Placemats

FINISHED SIZE: 13 x 18¹/₂in (33 x 47cm)

MATERIALS FOR EACH PLACEMAT
17 x 23in (43 x 58cm) 28-count
evenweave Jobelan in deep rose
17 x 23in (43 x 58cm) firm white
iron-on interfacing
Backing fabric, either more evenweave
or something that matches
Stranded floss as listed in
the key on page 83
Size 24 tapestry needle
Matching sewing thread

1. Mark the finished size of one place mat with basting. Overcast the edges.
2. See Fig. 2 for placement of the two charts. The embroidery is worked with two strands of floss over two threads of the fabric. Use a frame for this design.

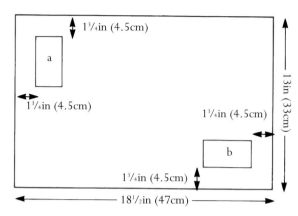

Fig. 2 Place mats showing placement of embroidery

3. When the embroidery is complete, iron the interfacing on the back.
4. Put the embroidered fabric and the backing right sides together. Machine stitch around all edges, leaving an opening so the work can be turned right side out. Trim the edges, turn, and press. Slip stitch to close the opening.

Variations

Use the individual tulips to decorate egg cozies, napkins, coasters, oven mitts, and the like.

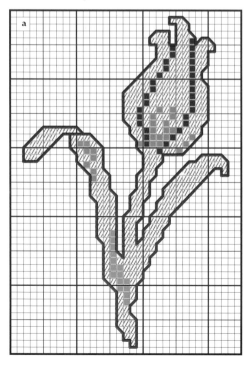

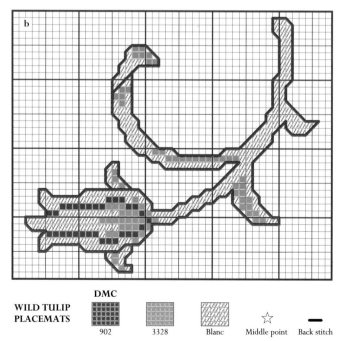

WILD TULIP PLACEMATS	DMC				
	902	3328	Blanc	☆ Middle point	▬ Back stitch

The Flower Garden Collection

This collection of items for the handbag includes a glasses case, checkbook cover, and credit card wallet. They are all worked on the same slate blue evenweave fabric and are decorated with details from the Flower Garden design — a stately, symmetrical design in woven silk, with a regular arrangement of large motifs. Between these, on a somewhat smaller scale, is a more informal arrangement of flowers and leaves that forms a network of ogee shapes around the dominant leaf motifs.

For my designs, I have selected snippets from the smaller-scale patterns. Although I have taken small details, the way that the shapes twist and turn, the look of the foliage, and the choice of color all produce an effect that is very strongly William Morris.

This is one of the designs where color is used absolutely flat, with no shading. Morris said he was aiming for the effect of inlaid metals in this design. And if you half-close your eyes, it is easy to see the copper, the gold, and the silver.

The Glasses Case.

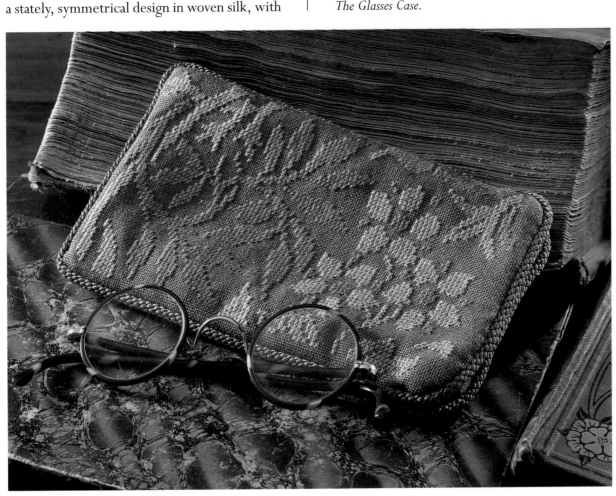

Checkbook Cover

Before you begin, measure the dimensions of the checkbook. Some are 3 x 7in (7.5 x 18cm), others are $3^1/4$ x $6^1/4$in (8 x 17cm). Some fold at the side, others at the top. Instructions here are for the slimmer, longer one with a side fold.

FINISHED SIZE: 3 x 7in (7.5 x 18cm)
STITCH COUNT: 43 x 94

MATERIALS
6 x 27in (15 x 69cm) 28-count evenweave
in denim blue
6 x 27in (15 x 69cm) medium-weight
iron-on interfacing
6 x 27in (15 x 69cm) thin lining material
Stranded floss as listed in the key on page 89
Size 24 tapestry needle
Matching sewing thread

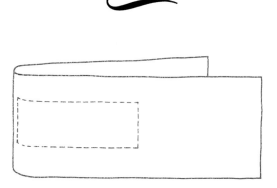

Fig. 1 Placement of embroidery.

1. Fold the fabric in half so that the shorter ends meet. Position the embroidery with its left-hand end just to the right of the fold (Fig. 1).
2. Work the embroidery with two strands of stranded floss over two threads of the fabric. A frame is advisable (see pages 117–118).
3. When you have finished, follow the instructions for making a book cover in (see page 124).

Credit Card Wallet

This design makes an attractive cover for one of the plastic wallets issued by banks or a case for a handbag mirror.

FINISHED SIZE: 3 x 4in (7.5 x 10cm)
STITCH COUNT: 40 x 54

MATERIALS
7 x 12in (18 x 30cm) 28-count evenweave
in denim blue
7 x 12in (18 x 30cm) medium-weight
iron-on interfacing
7 x 12in (18 x 30cm) thin lining material
Stranded floss as listed in the
key on page 89
Size 24 tapestry needle
Matching sewing thread

1. Fold the fabric in half and position the embroidery as shown below (Fig 2).
2. Work the embroidery with two strands of stranded floss over two threads of the fabric. A frame is advisable.
3. Finish by following the instructions for making a book cover, (see page 124).

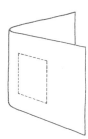

Fig. 2 Placement of embroidery.

Glasses Case

FINISHED SIZE: 3³/₄ x 6³/₄in (10 x 17cm)
STITCH COUNT: 52 x 94

MATERIALS
8 x 16in (20 x 41cm) 22-count evenweave
in denim blue
8 x 16in (20 x 41cm) medium-weight
iron-on interfacing
5 x 15in (13 x 38cm) lining material –
cotton velvet is good because it is soft and
quite thick; avoid anything too slippery
30in (76cm) lacing cord in a contrasting
color (optional)
Plastic canvas interlining (optional)
Stranded floss as listed in the
key on page 89
Size 24 tapestry needle
Matching sewing thread

1. Divide the fabric so that you have a piece 8 x 10in (20 x 25cm) to use for the embroidery. The remaining piece will be the backing. Mark the central horizontal and vertical guidelines with basting (see page 118).

2. Work the design using two strands of floss over two threads of the fabric. A frame is advisable (see pages 117–118).

3. When you have finished, remove the horizontal and vertical guidelines and press (see page 119). Iron the interfacing to the wrong side of the front and back pieces.

4. With right sides together, stitch about six threads outside the design. Leave the top ³/₄in (2cm) of each side and the top open. Trim to give rounded top corners.

5. Stitch a lining to fit inside. Slipstitch in place along the top edges. If you want to add a plastic interlining, cut it to fit inside the case. Overcast it around the edges and slip it between the outer fabric and the lining.

6. Slip stitch contrasting lacing cord around the edges, beginning at the top edge. Hide the end in the side seam. Take the cord along the top, down, and around, then across the other top edge before losing the other end in the other side seam (see Fig. 3).

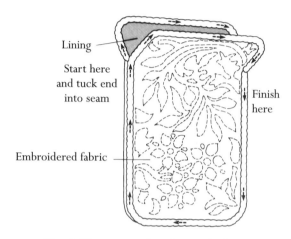

Fig. 3 Glasses case showing cord edging.

Detail of the Glasses Case.

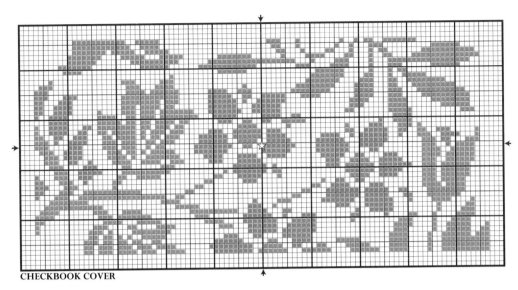

CHECKBOOK COVER

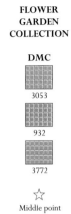
CREDIT CARD WALLET

FLOWER GARDEN COLLECTION KEY

Color	DMC	Anchor	Madeira
Green	3053(1)	858(1)	1510(1)
Blue	932(1)	1033(1)	1710(1)
Rust	3772(1)	1007(1)	2312(1)

One skein of each will be enough for all three items. These designs were embroidered using DMC threads. The alternatives may not be exact color equivalents.

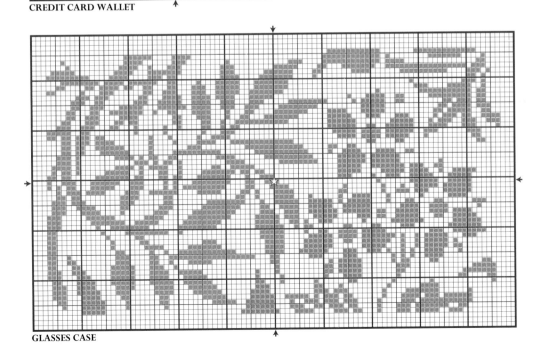

GLASSES CASE

89

The Tapestry Pictures

This project makes an attractive group of four flower pictures, all the same size. They are all worked on a subtle gray-green shade of Aida reminiscent of the dark backgrounds of Morris's tapestries. The flowers are Poppy, Bachelor's Button, Fritillary, and Campion. A complementary design and the Orange Tree Bellpull on page 100 are made up of branches of an orange tree, intertwined with acanthus leaves.

Morris and Co. tapestries are the inspiration for this group. The flowers are based on details picked out of a number of different tapestries – the Holy Grail, the Forest, and the Orchard. The same flowers appear over and over again. No matter what the subject of a Morris tapestry was, he liked to fill the background with trees and the foreground with flowers, after the style of the medieval millefleurs. Morris himself enjoyed designing the verdure areas, often leaving the figures to Edward Burne-Jones.

Morris loved flowers. At the Red House, he had designed a garden as well as the interior decorations. It was in the medieval style, divided by trellises and rose hedges and with an apple orchard and low beds of rosemary and lavender. Gardens were always important to him, but he reveled in the beauty of wildflowers as well. "The fields are all buttercuppy. The elms are mostly green up to their tops: the hawthorn not out, but the crabs beautiful."

The Tapestry Pictures (clockwise from left):
Fritillary, Poppy, Cornflower and White Campion.

In the tapestries, he concentrated on wild-flowers and treated them more naturalistically than in his repeating designs, where plants are often arranged as part of a geometric structure. However, there is still a degree of artificiality, as the flowers are chosen to fill different spaces and are arranged side by side, seldom overlapping even a leaf. The style owes much to the medieval tapestries Morris fell in love with as a student when he first visited France. "No word can tell you how its mingled beauty, history, and romance took hold of me: I can only say that looking back on my past life, I find it was the greatest pleasure I have ever had," he wrote. Another influence was the old herbals he used for his research. These books were illustrated with woodcut images that managed to arrange a plant within a rectangular block in such a way that habit, leaves, flowers, fruit, or seeds, and sometimes roots as well, could all be clearly seen.

The flowers I have selected have been simplified slightly, and I have made them all about the same size. The character and coloring are authentic, although the choice of the green background caused me some headaches when choosing green thread for the leaves. It is essential to have a very dark accent, but the other greens need to be pale enough to contrast with the Aida. I have chosen a number of colors that are common to several of the designs to increase the unity of the group.

The Poppy

This makes a glorious splash of color against the dark green. It is the common field poppy, sometimes called the corn poppy, Flanders poppy. Its seeds can besprinkled on bread, and the petals were once used in a cough syrup.

FINISHED SIZE: to fit a 10- x 10-in
(25 x 25cm) frame
STITCH COUNT: 125 x 125

MATERIALS
14 x 14in (36 x 36cm)16-count
Aida in bay leaf green
Stranded floss as listed in the
key on page 96
Size 26 tapestry needle

1. Mark the central horizontal and vertical guidelines with basting (see page 118).
2. Start to embroider by following the stalk that runs along the center line. Use two strands of floss over one block of the fabric. From there, work outward, counting carefully.
3. When you make the leaves, you will find that some areas along their spines are left blank. This allows the green background fabric, which is just the right color, to show through.
4. When you have finished, remove the guidelines and press (see page 119).

Cornflower

The cornflower, or batchelor's button, is another species that was once common in fields but is now much rarer as a result of weedkillers. It is a flower that has delighted painters and embroiderers through the centuries, though Gerard's *Herbal*, of which Morris had a copy, says: "In the fields it hindreth and annoyeth the Reapers, by dulling and turning the edges of their sickles in reaping of corne." Its petals were used for pigment and were considered to have medicinal benefits for the eyes.

FINISHED SIZE: to fit a 10 x 10in
(25 x 25cm) frame
STITCH COUNT: 107 x 124

MATERIALS
14 x 14in (35 x 35cm)16-count
Aida in bay leaf green
Stranded floss as listed in the
key on page 97
Size 26 tapestry needle

1. Mark the central horizontal and vertical guidelines with basting (see see page 118).
2. Start to embroider around the central cross, using two strands of floss over one block of fabric. Begin with the palest green and embroider the edge of the leaf that coincides with the central cross. From there, go to the top of the central stem, then work the stem of the right-hand flower.
3. If you then change to the next green and work the stem of the left-hand flower, you will begin to have a framework to work from. From there, work out, counting carefully.
4. When you have finished, remove the guidelines and press (see page 119).

The Fritillary

The snake's head fritillary used to flower abundantly in British meadows, especially in the valley along the River Thames, where Morris spent much of his life at Oxford University and at Kelmscott Manor. It was formerly called the Ginny-Hen Floure because its petals resemble the plumage of a guinea fowl.

Today, however, it is more likely to be seen cultivated in flowerbeds, where its unusual checkered petals make it a very decorative addition to a border.

FINISHED SIZE: to fit a 10 x 10in
(25 x 25cm) frame
STITCH COUNT: 121 x 125

MATERIALS
14 x 14in (35 x 35cm) 16-count Zweigart
Aida in Bay Leaf green
Stranded floss as listed in the
key on page 98
Size 26 tapestry needle

1. Mark the central horizontal and vertical guidelines with basting (see page 118).
2. Start to embroider around the central cross, using two strands of floss over one block of fabric. Begin with the bluer green, and embroider the leaf that coincides with the central cross. From there, work down the stem attached to it. Continuing with the same color, work the leaf to its right and the others on the same side. This way, you begin to build up a framework, which makes it easier to find your place. From there, work out, counting carefully.
3. When you have finished, remove the guidelines and press (see page 119).

The White Campion

The the flower of the white campion opens in the evening to attract the moths. Its close relation, the red campion, was often grown in English Tudor gardens. I like the contrast of the pale leaves and flowers with the dark background, and the deliberate, decorative way they have been arranged.

FINISHED SIZE: to fit a 10- x 10-in
(25 x 25cm) frame
STITCH COUNT: 124 x 124

MATERIALS
14 x 14in (35 x 35cm) 16-count
Aida in bay leaf green
Stranded floss as listed in the
key on page 95
Size 26 tapestry needle

1. Mark the central horizontal and vertical guidelines with basting (see page 118).
2. Start to embroider around the central cross, using two strands of floss over one block of the fabric. Begin with the pale green and embroider the central stem and leaves. Continuing with the same color, work the stems to the left and right. This way you begin to build up a framework which makes it easier to find your place. From there, work out, counting carefully.
3. When you have finished, remove the guidelines and press (see page 119).

Variations

1. I have chosen 10-in square (25cm) frames for the group, but a mat with a circular window in a larger frame would also look attractive.
2. Vary the size of the design by using a different count of fabric. This color (No. 626) is also available in 18-count Aida, 32-count Belfast linen, and 28-count Brittney and Quaker cloth. It is called bay leaf where it refers to Aida, and antique green where it refers to evenweave fabric.
3. Using the 28-count fabric, worked over two threads, the design would be suitable for a 14-in (36cm) pillow.

POPPY
1. Select just a part of the design, perhaps the left and center flower and the two buds, to decorate small items like a needlebook or pincushion. A single flower would enhance a key ring or refrigerator magnet.

CORNFLOWER
1. Try using the central flower, its upper two leaves, and stem to decorate a bookmark. If you want a longer design, you can repeat that motif upside down, overlapping the stems.
2. Use individual flower heads to decorate coasters or to scatter over larger areas.

FRITILLARY
1. Pick out single flowers with attached leaves for use on greeting cards.

WHITE CAMPION
1. Select sprigs of the plant to use for cards and small items such as needlebooks.

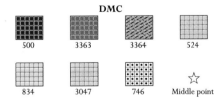

WHITE CAMPION

DMC

500	3363	3364	524

834	3047	746	☆ Middle point

WHITE CAMPION KEY

Color	DMC	Anchor	Madeira
Cream	746(1)	275(1)	0101(1)
Light Yellow	3047(1)	852(1)	2205(1)
Darker yellow	834(1)	874(1)	2204(1)
Dark green	500(1)	683(1)	1705(1)
Pale willow green	524(1)	858(1)	1511(1)
Yellow-green	3364(1)	260(1)	1603(1)
Olive green	3363(1)	262(1)	1602(1)

The White Campion design was stitched using DMC threads. The alternatives may not be exact color equivalents. Quantities are shown in parentheses.

POPPY

DMC

500	3816	3817	834
3371	3328	758	☆ Middle point

POPPY KEY

Color	DMC	Anchor	Madeira
Red	3328(1)	1024(1)	0406(1)
Pink	758(1)	9575(1)	0403(1)
Dark brown	3371(1)	382(1)	2004(1)
Yellow	834(1)	874(1)	2204(1)
Dark green	500(1)	683(1)	1705(1)
Pale green	3817(1)	875(1)	1702(1)
Blue-green	3816(1)	876(1)	1703(1)

The Poppy design was stitched using DMC threads. The alternatives may not be exact color equivalents. Quantities are shown in parentheses.

CORNFLOWER

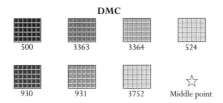

DMC

| 500 | 3363 | 3364 | 524 |

| 930 | 931 | 3752 | ☆ Middle point |

CORNFLOWER

Color	DMC	Anchor	Madeira
Pale blue	3752(1)	1032(1)	1710(1)
Mid blue	931(1)	1034(1)	1711(1)
Dark blue	930(1)	1035(1)	1712(1)
Dark green	500(1)	683(1)	1705(1)
Pale willow green	524(1)	858(1)	1511(1)
Yellow-green	3364(1)	260(1)	1603(1)
Olive green	3363(1)	262(1)	1602(1)

The Bachelor's Button design was stitched using DMC threads. The alternatives may not be exact color equivalents. quantities are shown in parentheses.

FRITILLARY

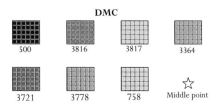

DMC

500	3816	3817	3364
3721	3778	758	☆ Middle point

FRITILLARY KEY

Color	DMC	Anchor	Madeira
Pale pink	758(1)	9575(1)	0403(1)
Medium pink	3778(1)	1013(1)	0402(1)
Dark pink	3721(1)	896(1)	0602(1)
Dark green	500(1)	683(1)	1705(1)
Pale green	3817(1)	875(1)	1701(1)
Yellow-green	3364(1)	260(1)	1603(1)
Blue-green	3816(1)	876(1)	1703(1)

The Fritillary design was stitched using DMC threads. The alternatives may not be exact color equivalents. Qunatities are shown in parentheses.

The Orange Tree Bellpull

he inspiration for this bellpull is the "Angeli Laudantes" (Praising Angels) tapestry, which shows two figures of angels by Burne-Jones. Typical Burne-Jones figures, tall and elegant with soulful faces, they are dressed in lavish blue-and-gold draperies and have flaming red wings. Both carry harps. The entire background is dark but filled with flowers, and around the field of flowers is a border of leaves, flowers, and fruit.

It is the border that I have concentrated on for this design. It is composed of large acanthus leaves coiling up the tapestry, showing a greener and a bluer side alternately, and forming a sort of zigzag. The spaces in between are filled with orange fruit or flowers and leaves. I have chosen a typical section and finished it off at top and bottom with the curled leaves that are used at the corners of the border.

The tapestry is in a style we associate strongly with William Morris, but in this case we should say Morris and Co. By the time this tapestry was woven in 1894, Morris was occupied with the Kelmscott Press, and Henry Dearle was responsible for the tapestry production. Dearle had no formal training in an art school and was the product of Morris's belief in the old system of master teaching apprentice. When Morris relocated the company to Merton Abbey, Dearle was put in charge and he shared his skill and experience with other apprentices in the tapestry workshops. He took an active part in the design work, being particularly good at the verdure and the floral back-

grounds. "Angeli Laudantes" is a combination of the Burne-Jones design (originally drawn for a stained-glass window for Salisbury Cathedral) and a background by Dearle.

The bellpull brings together the color schemes of all the tapestry pictures. The different colors of foliage are represented in the acanthus leaves, and the reds of Poppy and Fritillary and yellow and white of the Campion are all represented in the orange flowers and fruit.

FINISHED SIZE: 6 x 29$\frac{1}{2}$in (15 x 75cm)
STITCH COUNT: 66 x 400

MATERIALS
10 x 36in (25 x 91cm) 16-count
Aida in bay leaf green
Stranded floss as listed in the
key on page 101
Size 26 tapestry needle
6-in (15cm) bellpull ends
6$\frac{1}{2}$ x 30in (17 x 76cm) dark iron-on or
sew-in interfacing
Lining material, slightly larger, in a dark color
2yd (1.8m) cord to finish long edges

1. Make a color palette with a piece of cardboard punched down the edges. Attach an example of each color and write the number against it. Group the first four greens separately from the next four, grading the groups from light to dark.
2. Mark a guideline down the center of the length. Mark another at the center horizontally, and thereafter every 50 squares up and down.
3. Work the embroidery, using two strands of floss over one block of Aida.
4. When you have finished, remove the guidelines and press (see page 119).
5. Mark the finished size you require with pins or basting. This will depend on the bellpull ends

THE ORANGE TREE BELLPULL

you choose. Be sure to leave enough at the top and bottom to fold around the bellpull ends (see Fig. 1).

6. Iron or baste the interfacing to the back of the bell-pull.

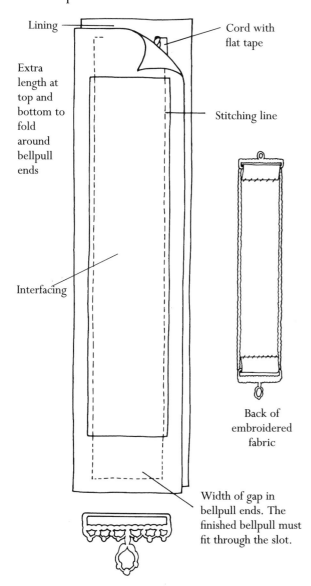

Fig 1 Constructing the bellpull.

7. Place the lining material and embroidery right sides together and pin. Stitch all around, except for an opening along the top to allow you to turn the bellpull right side out. Slip stitch the opening closed and press the seams.

8. Choose an upholstery cord to finish the long

edges. Hand-stitch it to the edges, hiding the ends in the side seams in the turned-over area. (If you have bought cord with a flat tape that is included in the seam, layer it, cord inward, between the embroidery and the lining before you stitch them together.)

9. Finish the ends with bellpull hardware, following the manufacturer's directions.

Variations

1. Vary the size of the design slightly by varying the count of fabric.

2. If you require a longer bellpull, you could repeat the zigzags of acanthus before you add the finishing curled leaf. To do this, photocopy the chart several times and then try cutting it across just below the top curl and adding two more leaves.

BELLPULL KEY

Color	DMC	Anchor	Madeira
Rust	356 (1)	5975 (1)	0402 (1)
Peach	352 (1)	9575 (1)	0403 (1)
Cream	746 (1)	275 (1)	0101 (1)
Yellow	3822 (1)	295 (1)	109 (1)
Very pale blue-green	927 (1)	848 (1)	1708 (1)
Pale blue-green	926 (2)	850 (2)	1707 (2)
Blue-green	3768 (2)	779 (2)	1706 (2)
Dark green	500 (2)	683 (2)	1705 (2)
Pale willow green	524 (1)	858 (1)	1511 (1)
Yellow-green	3364 (3)	260 (3)	1603 (3)
Olive green	3363 (3)	263 (3)	1602 (3)
Dark olive	520 (1)	862 (1)	1514 (1)

The bellpull was stitched with DMC threads. The alternatives may not be exact color equivalents. Quantities are given in parentheses.

THE ORANGE TREE BELLPULL

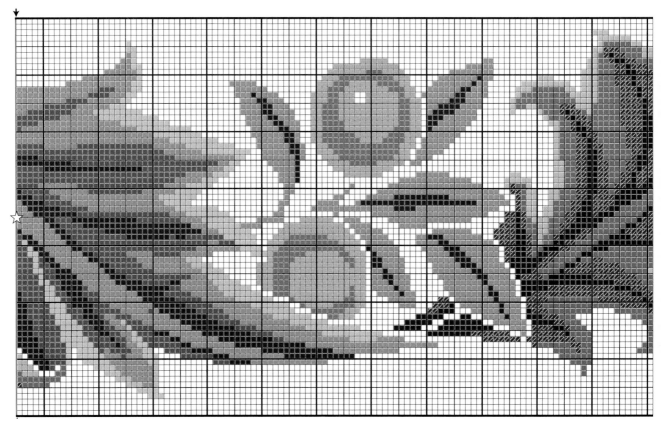

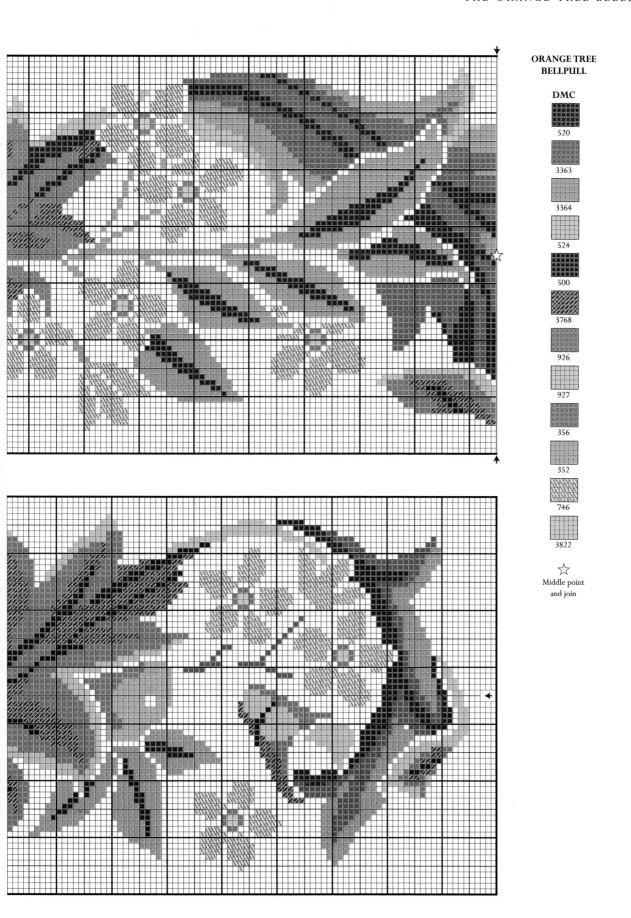

**ORANGE TREE
BELLPULL**

DMC

520

3363

3364

524

500

3768

926

927

356

352

746

3822

☆
Middle point
and join

Kennet Dresser Set

These delicate designs are based on the Kennet fabric, one of a series named after tributaries of the river Thames. The dresser cloth is embroidered in pale pinks on white, which is reversed in the designs for a hairbrush and a mirror back and for the lid of a crystal bowl.

William Morris frequently combined two very different scales in his designs. This one, from the 1880s, shows a series of meandering branches bearing bold leaves and flowers. But it is the small-scale monochrome decoration he used between the branches that inspired my designs. All the spaces are filled with a coiling foliage pattern, reminiscent of medieval manuscript painting and of Tudor embroidery, which in some places bears rose leaves and flowers, and in others vine leaves and grapes. The dresser cloth uses the rose motif in the center and the vine leaves and tendrils at the ends. The brush and mirror backs show a simplified version of the rose motif.

The Kennet design was produced as a printed chintz and as a woven silk. The printed version shows the coiling motifs in white on a dark indigo blue background, but the silks have more delicate color schemes. In one, the motifs are pale yellow on a darker yellow background, and another is white on pink, which I have used in the brush and mirror backs.

Because I wanted to use the design on both a large and a small scale, I have chosen different counts of evenweave fabric. To make the design

The Kennet Dresser Cloth on which is placed (from left) *the Crystal Bowl Lid, the Mirror and Hairbrush.*

contrast with the pretty pink background fabric of the smaller pieces, I have chosen a mixture of white stranded floss and blending filament. This adds a different texture and a reflectivity that is attractive when picked up by candle-light, something Morris considered when choosing colors. If you do not like the shimmer, I suggest substituting white flower thread for a matte effect.

In William Morris's design, all the small-scale detail is in a single color. I decided to add the pink shade to the rose centers to link with the roses on the cloth. I also added the same color spots to the background in a fashion that Morris often employed in his designs.

Dresser Cloth

FINISHED SIZE: 12 x 25½in (30 x 65cm), plus lace edging
STITCH COUNT: 76 x 216

MATERIALS
16 x 30in (41 x 76cm) 21-count evenweave
Jobelan in white
Stranded floss as listed on the key on page 107
Size 22 tapestry needle
2½-yd (3m) 2-in wide (5cm) heavy
lace edging

KENNET DRESSER CLOTH	DMC	760	761	819	☆ Middle point

1. Begin by overcasting the edges, by hand or with a wide zigzag on the machine, to prevent the fabric from fraying.

2. It is advisable to use a frame when stitching evenweave (see page 117).

3. Mark the central horizontal and vertical guidelines with basting (see page 118).

4. Embroider the design, using three strands at a time and working over two threads.

5. When you have stitched the central motif, it is helpful to add a guideline 75 stitches to left and right of center to position the end motifs.

6. When you have finished, mark the finished size. Stitch around outside this line, using a fairly closely stitched wide zigzag in white thread.

Trim the fabric away around the edge, close to the stitching, and turn the edges under. Pin the lace in place on top, close to the fold, gathering it just at the corners to fit. Make the seam in the lace coincide with a gathered corner. Machine-stitch close to the edge.

Dresser cloth key

Color	DMC	Anchor	Madeira
Pale pink	819 (2)	271 (2)	0501 (2)
Medium pink	761 (1)	1022 (1)	0404 (1)
Darker pink	760 (1)	1023 (1)	0406 (1)

The sample was embroidered using the DMC thread. The alternatives will be a slightly different color. Quantities are given in parentheses.

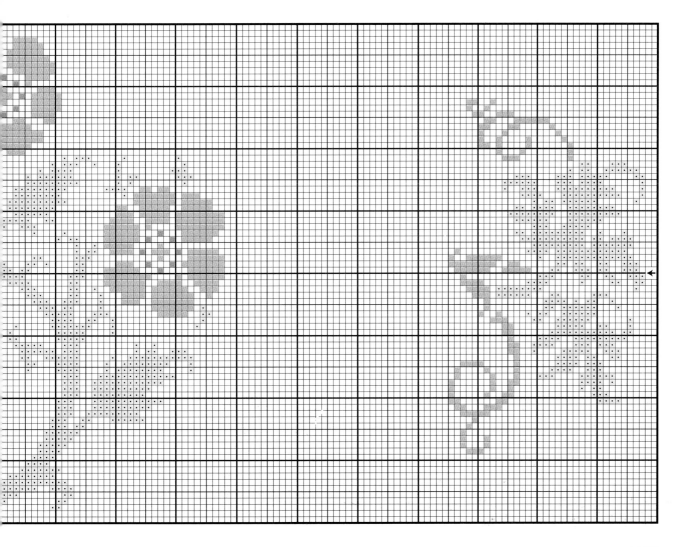

HAIRBRUSH AND MIRROR BACKS

**KENNET
DRESSER SET**

DMC

760

819

5200+4300
Blending thread

☆
Middle point

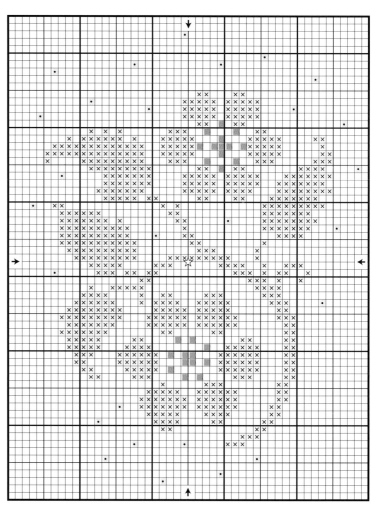

CRYSTAL BOWL

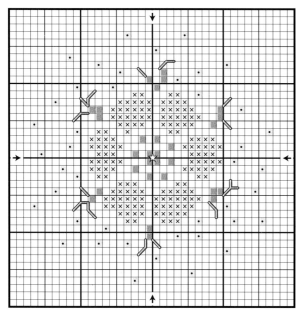

HAIRBRUSH, MIRROR BACKS, AND CRYSTAL BOWL KEY

Color	DMC	Anchor	Madeira
Pale pink	819 (1)	271 (1)	0501 (1)
Darker pink	760 (1)	1023 (1)	0405 (1)
White	5200 (1)	1 (1)	White (1)
Pearl	4300 (1)	032 (1)	000 (1)
	Blending thread	Kreinik blending filament	Rainbow blending thread

These designs were stitched using DMC stranded floss and Kreinik blending filament. If you substitute one of the blending threads, use just one strand with the floss. The alternative floss will be a slightly different color.

A matte alternative to the white and pearl combination would be to use DMC white flower thread (two skeins).

Quantities are given in parentheses. These amounts are enough for the brush and mirror backs and the crystal bowl.

Hairbrush and Mirror Backs

DESIGN SIZE: about 3 x 4in (8 x 10cm)
STITCH COUNT: 46 x 58

MATERIALS

12 x 12in (30 x 30 cm) or 9 x 18in
(23 x 46cm) 28-count evenweave Jobelan
in ash rose
White medium-weight iron-on interfacing to
match fabric size
Stranded floss as listed in the
key on page 108
Pearl blending filament
Size 24 tapestry needle
Silver-plated hairbrush and mirror kit
size of brush back $3^1/2$in x $4^1/2$in (9 x 11.5cm),
size of mirror back
$4^3/4$ x $5^3/4$in (12 cm x 15cm)

1. Overcast the edges, by hand or with a wide zigzag on the machine, to prevent fraying.
2. It is advisable to use a frame when stitching evenweave (see page 117).
3. This piece of fabric will be enough for the brush, mirror backs, and crystal bowl lid. Work them on the same piece, but space them apart, leaving room to cut them out.
4. Mark the central horizontal and vertical guidelines in basting for each design (see page 118). The brush and mirror are worked from the same chart, but leave more room around the mirror design because the frame is larger.
5. Embroider the design over two threads of the fabric. For the pinks, use two strands at a time; for the white, use two strands of floss plus two strands of blending filament.
6. When you have finished, remove the guide-

lines and press gently (see page 119). Iron on the interfacing, cut oversize. Now mark the exact size, using the manufacturer's templates provided with the brush and mirror and cut them out with sharp scissors. When you cut out the embroidery for the brush, be sure the white stitching is close to the top end of the frame. Let $^1/2$in (1cm) of background fabric show above the white petal.
7. Mount in the brush and mirror according to the manufacturer's instructions.

Crystal Bowl

FINISHED SIZE: $2^1/2$in (6cm) diameter
STITCH COUNT: 34 x 32

MATERIALS

$3^1/2$-in (9cm) diameter glass crystal bowl with
silver-plated lid rim kit
If you make only this item, you will need the
following: (Otherwise there will be enough
left over from the brush and mirror backs).
6 x 6in (15 x 15cm) 28-count Jobelan
in ash rose
6 x 6in (15 x 15cm) white medium-weight
iron-on interfacing
Stranded floss as listed in the key on page 108
Pearl blending filament
Size 24 tapestry needle

1. Prepare the fabric and work the embroidery by following the instructions for the brush and mirror backs, using the relevant chart opposite.
2. Remove the guidelines and press gently (see page 119). Iron on the interfacing and cut the fabric to the size specified in the instructions accompanying the bowl.
3. Mount the embroidery in the bowl lid according to the manufacturer's instructions.

The Brer Rabbit Picture

This intricate picture would look attractive in many places around the house, but I think there will be strong pressure from children to hang it in their room. I have used a great variety of effects in this design. For the rabbits, I chose shades of Marlitt for its silky texture. For the foliage and flowers, I blended fine metallic braid next to Marlitt, next to stranded floss with blending filament. That combination has effect which alters subtly as the light changes.

This design is based on Morris's printed cotton fabric named after the Uncle Remus stories about Brer Rabbit, which he remembered reading with pleasure to his daughters. It is another example of his symmetrical "turn over" designs and was produced as a monochrome design in pale blue on a darker indigo blue ground. There was a fashion for blue-and-white designs at the time, fueled largely by the new imports of china from Japan.

Suitable as the monochrome is for a background fabric, I felt it needed livening up to make a picture. I have kept the dark blue background and restricted the coloring to the blue segment of the color circle, but veered toward the purple and the green.

The original design is basically a rectangular grid with the uprights formed by the oak trees and the horizontals by the rabbit groups. It shows a pair of rabbits hiding under enormous acanthus leaves, with little flowers all around them. From between them springs the trunk of an oak tree, which bears decoratively arranged oak leaves and acorns. In Morris's design a secondary pair of birds interlocks with the rabbit

group and fills in the space between acanthus leaves and oak leaves, but I felt that my picture was complete without them.

FINISHED SIZE: 14 x 20in (35.5 x 51cm)
STITCH COUNT: 234 x 168

MATERIALS
18 x 24in (46 x 61cm) 14-count Aida in navy blue
Anchor Marlitt, Anchor stranded floss, fine braid, blending filament, as listed in the key on page 113
Size 24 tapestry needle

1. Mark the central horizontal and vertical guidelines with basting (see page 118). It is advisable to add guidelines at 30 squares to right and left, and at 30, 60, and 90 squares up and down to help keep your place in the design.

2. The design is worked over one block of the fabric, using the thread or mixture of threads described in the key on page 113. Because so many threads are used, it is sensible to use a frame (see page 117); otherwise, you may find some areas are pulled tighter than others.

3. Embroider carefully, checking your position against the guidelines. When working with a mixture of threads, try to pull them evenly and make certain that there are no loops left behind on the back.

4. The navy blue area that outlines the eye can be left as the background fabric. Or if you prefer, it can be filled in with blending filament to give an extra gleam.

5. When you have embroidered the design, remove the guidelines and press (see page 119).

6. Frame the picture as required, see instructions on page 122.

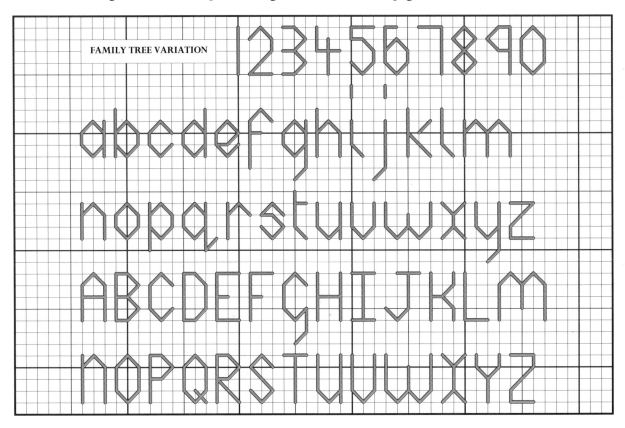

FAMILY TREE VARIATION

Variations

1. Instead of framing the picture, mount it using the decorative top and tail pieces available which are like elongated bellpull ends.

2. Worked on a larger piece of fabric or a coarser (lower) count of fabric, this design also makes a very handsome firescreen. Navy is available in a wide choice of fabrics.

3. Make the central oak tree a kind of family tree for recording the birth of children or

grandchildren. Photocopy the chart and cut across one square above the center. Figure out how much extra space you will need — as a rough guide, at least 10 squares per entry and 10 in between. Add in the required amount of

extra trunk, and on each side record names and birthdays. Use threads chosen from the line used in the design. A simple backstitch alphabet and set of numbers have been charted on page 112 to help you. Do not try to work this piece without drafting the design on graph paper with a pencil eraser first. If you choose this option, do not forget to use a longer piece of fabric.

4. Work just the bottom half of the design. Cut the picture off before the tree divides for the first oak leaf. You could add more mauve flowers to fill the top corners.

BRER RABBIT KEY

Color	Thread	Strands	Skeins/spools
RABBITS			
White	Marlitt 800	2	1
Pale blue	Marlitt 1009	2	2
Darker blue	Marlitt 835	2	1
Eye blue (optional)	Kreinik blending filament 051HL	3	1
FLOWERS AND LEAVES			
Mauve	Marlitt 1007	2	1
Purple	Kreinik fine braid 012	1	1
Turquoise	Kreinik fine braid 029	1	2
Star blue	Kreinik fine braid 094	1	1
Wedgwood blue	Kreinik fine braid 622	1	2
Blue ice	Kreinik fine braid 1432	1	2
Sky blue	Marlitt 1053	2	1
Outer leaf	Kreinik blending filament 006/	2	2
	Anchor stranded 1039	1	1
Light oak leaf	Kreinik blending filament 006/	2	
	Anchor stranded 185	1	1
Med. oak leaf	Marlitt 1066	2	1
Dark oak leaf	Marlitt 1067	2	1

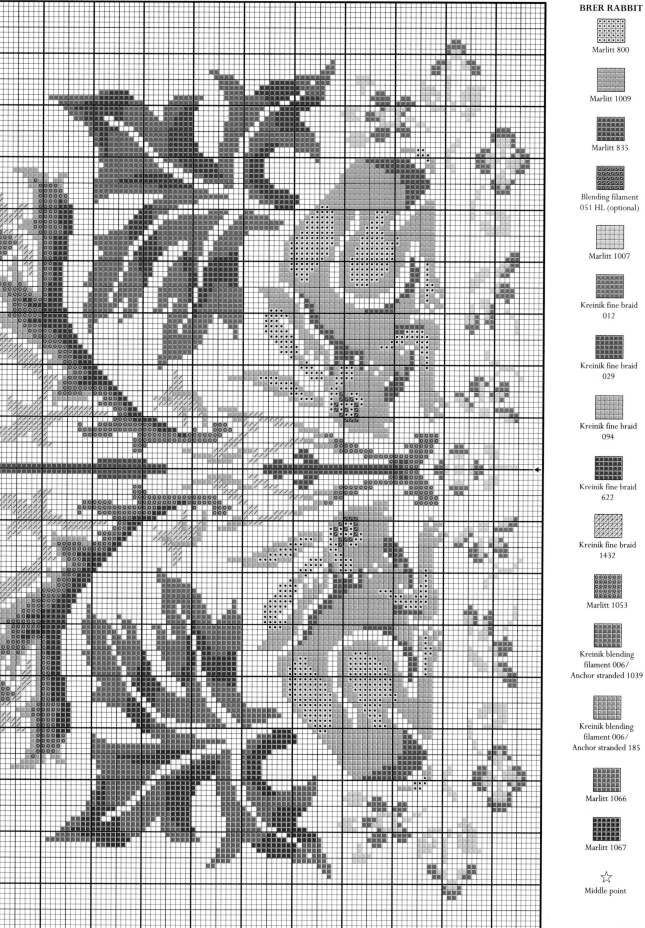

Marlitt 800

Marlitt 1009

Marlitt 835

Blending filament
051 HL (optional)

Marlitt 1007

Kreinik fine braid
012

Kreinik fine braid
029

Kreinik fine braid
094

Kreinik fine braid
622

Kreinik fine braid
1432

Marlitt 1053

Kreinik blending
filament 006/
Anchor stranded 1039

Kreinik blending
filament 006/
Anchor stranded 185

Marlitt 1066

Marlitt 1067

☆
Middle point

Basic Techniques

The following suggestions are for your guidance only. They are not hard-and-fast rules, and if you have figured out a way that suits you better, by all means stick to it. Those who have not done much embroidery before, however, may find the following pages useful.

Fabrics

Each of the projects in this book states exactly the fabric needed for working the piece as shown in the accompanying photograph. I have deliberately chosen a wide variety of fabrics, but there is of course no reason why you should not use different fabrics rather than the ones specified if you prefer.

BLOCKWEAVE FABRICS

The blockweave fabrics such, as Aida, are probably the simplest to work. The weave locks each block of threads in place, giving a very stable, firm fabric. Hardanger fabric, used for the bowl lids on page 67, is very similar. Silk gauze is woven in an interlock fashion, which means that although the threads are very thin, the method of working is, in fact, just the same as with Aida. Plastic canvas and perforated paper are two more materials where the "threads" are locked together.

EVENWEAVE FABRICS

"Evenweave" just means that there are the same number of warp threads as weft threads to the inch. Manufacturers use the thread count to differentiate between the size of fabrics, and the higher the number, the more threads or blocks of thread there are to the inch. Evenweave is usually embroidered over two threads at a time. Thus a 28-count evenweave fabric can be substituted for a 14-count Aida, a 32-count evenweave for a 16-count Aida, and vice versa. Just two of the projects use evenweave worked over one thread (see pages 41 and 42).

CALCULATING THE DESIGN SIZE

As you gain confidence, you may choose to work on a larger or smaller count of fabric. This will of course result in the finished piece being a slightly different size.

To find out how large a piece would become, divide the stitch count given by the number of threads per inch of the fabric. For example, the Flower Pendant (page 41) has a stitch count of 39 x 39. If we call this 40 x 40, it will make calculation easier. It is worked on 30-count silk gauze. Dividing 40 by 30 threads to the inch, we obtain a size of $1\frac{1}{3}$ inches. If instead we decide to work it on 14-count Aida, we would get a size of nearly 3 inches (40 ÷ 14). The calculation for evenweave fabric takes just a little longer because evenweave is usually worked over two threads. If we decide to work on 32-count linen, we would start by dividing 32 by 2 = 16. The size would be $2\frac{1}{2}$ inches (40 ÷ 16).

Do the same calculation for the length and the width to find the new size. If you decide to work a design on a different fabric, remember that all the designs need a margin of plain fabric around the motif. In addition, it is wise to add an extra 2in (5cm) on all sides to allow for framing. The amounts of fabric specified in the projects have included these calculations.

WASTE CANVAS

Some of the alternative suggestions refer to "waste canvas." This is a stiff canvas, which can be obtained in different counts. It is used where a small motif is wanted on clothing or furnishings that are not made from fabrics with an eavenweave composition. It is basted over the fabric where the motif is required and gives a regular mesh to work cross stitches on. When complete, the threads of the waste canvas are pulled out from the edges with tweezers. This is easier if the canvas is slightly damp.

Threads

Many of the projects described use stranded floss, with which most people are familiar. Divide them into lengths of about 20in (50cm) and divide each length into its six strands. Recombine the number needed. Marlitt is a four-stranded thread that is treated in the same way. Madeira metallic gold No.5 has slightly twisted threads, which also can be divided into individual strands, though is not necessary in the project that uses it. Pearl cotton and metallic braid are used just as they are, and blending filament and thread are usually employed in conjunction with stranded cottons. I just thread a length along with the floss, but manufacturers recommend other ways of knotting the thread to the needle and you may wish to try some of them.

The number of skeins or spools of thread needed is stated on the key for each project, in parentheses after each color.

Needles

All the embroidery is done with blunt-ended tapestry needles. I have recommended sizes, but you may prefer a different size. The matter of size is a compromise between having an eye large enough to take the thread and a needle that will pass through the holes without too much friction. If you leave the needle in the fabric, make sure it is at the edge in case it leaves marks.

General Accessories

In addition to fabric, thread, and needles, you must have a good pair of embroidery scissors with sharp points, and fabric-cutting scissors as well. And I think that a bright light is essential; many are made especially for embroidery, but a studio-type light is perfectly adequate. It is important to position the light correctly. If you want to work in an easy chair rather than at a table, the light should be positioned so that your body does not throw a shadow over the work.

When you are working on dark fabrics, it is very helpful to place a brightly reflective sheet of paper or a white pillowcase over your knees. Either will make the holes in the fabric show up much more clearly.

Working on the designs for this book, especially the brooches and pendants, has made me appreciate the value of a magnifier; I would not be without one now. The kind that hang around the neck are reasonbly priced; some embroidery lights have magnifiers attached.

Embroidery frames

It is very tempting to start the piece without wasting time setting up an embroidery frame, and it is certainly much easier to roll up the fabric and move it around with you if it is not framed. Remember: Never fold the work up, because the creases can be really difficult to deal with later.

My recommendation is to use a frame for any evenweave fabric or when you are working with a mixture of threads, for you may find that their different characteristics cause you to pull some threads more firmly than others.

HOOPS

For small pieces, a hoop (see Fig. 1) or spring frame hoop (see Fig. 2) is suitable. Always try to

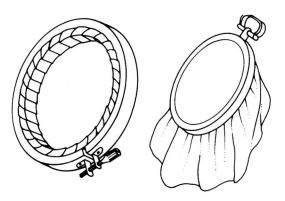

Fig. 1 Hoop. **Fig. 2** Spring frame hoop.

use a hoop large enough to take the whole of the design. If that is not possible, leave the hoop on the work only while you are actually stitching. When repositioning the work do not let the hoop edge coincide with an embroidered area.

SCROLL FRAMES

For larger pieces, a rectangular scroll frame (see Fig. 3) is the traditional answer. The embroidery fabric is stitched to a tape attached to the top and bottom rods, matching the center of the tape to the center of the fabric. The frame has wing nuts that can be loosened to allow the rods to rotate to roll the fabric up if it is larger than the frame, like the Bellpull. The edges are then laced to the sides of the frame. This type of frame gives very good firm support and is particularly suitable if the embroidery is to be left in the frame for any length of time.

Match center marks

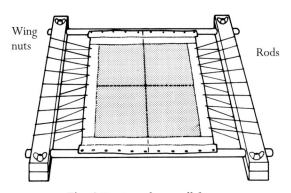

Wing nuts

Rods

Fig. 3 Rectangular scroll frame.

CLIP FRAMES

A recent introduction is the rectangular clip frame made from lengths of plastic tube (see Fig. 4). These come with different lengths of tube, which are assembled with the help of plastic corner pieces. The fabric is placed over the tubes and clipped in place with half-tubes, which are slit along their length. This kind of frame is particularly suitable where part of a large volume of fabric is being worked (for example, the tablecloth on page 72).

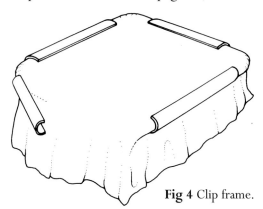

Fig 4 Clip frame.

To Begin

Although it is tempting simply to thread your needle and begin to stitch, you may find that you soon encounter difficulties. These problems can easily be avoided by following the simple advice given below.

PREPARING THE FABRIC

When I am working on Aida, I find that cutting it out with pinking shears is enough to stop it from fraying. I like to edge evenweave by using a machine zigzag stitch, though overcasting the edges by hand is equally successful.

Center lines are shown on the charts by the use of opposing arrows. In addition, the central point is marked by a star. Find the center of your fabric by folding it in half both ways. Mark the center lines with sewing thread, using a basting stitch. Make sure, especially when you are using evenweave, that the line of stitches is straight along the grain of the fabric. In some of the larger designs, I have suggested marking extra guidelines; choose a different color for these.

FOLLOWING THE CHARTS

Each colored square on the charts represents one cross stitch. The colors used for the charts are often an exaggeration of the thread color so that there is no confusion. In some cases, I have used very similar shades in the embroidery, and so occasionally a symbol has been added to help you to identify which thread to use. Where backstitch is used, it is represented by a thick colored line. The chart shows slightly more pronounced grid lines after every ten squares to help you to count.

You may want to use the charts straight from the book, but if you prefer, you can photocopy them in color for your own use (which allows you to enlarge or reduce them). You can then cross off areas as you work them, which you may find helpful. Photocopying also lets you draw the center lines and any extra guidelines with a felt-tip pen to match the lines you have worked. You can also use magnetic markers, available from craft stores, to help you locate the area of the chart you are working on. As a rule, I start embroidering at the center and work blocks of one color at a time.

Although this book is devoted to cross stitch, the charts could also be used for needlepoint – simply use half cross stitch or petit point (tent stitch) instead of cross stitch. Remember, though, that you will need to add a background color. The only charts unsuitable are those that rely heavily on backstitch, such as the Wild Tulip design on page 80.

STARTING TO STITCH

To begin stitching in an empty area of fabric, knot the thread and take it through the fabric from the front ¹/₂in (1cm) from the point where you wish to begin. When you have stitched over the thread, the knot can be trimmed off and the end worked through to the back. To start a new thread in a stitched area, just thread it under four or five stitches on the back of the work before starting to stitch.

To Finish

To finish off an area of stitching, thread your needle back through the last four or five stitches on the wrong side of the fabric. This eliminates the lumps that could spoil the look of the finished piece.

PRESSING

When you finish a piece of embroidery, it will need careful pressing; the objective is to smooth out the fabric and correct any distortion without flattening the stitches and spoiling the texture. A towel covered with a sheet or pillowcase should give a soft enough surface on which to rest the embroidery. Lay the embroidery face down, pull it into shape, making sure the grain of the fabric is straight, and press it gently on the back at a heat suitable for the type of fabric and thread. If you use steam, you will find that Aida becomes quite pliable; it can be pulled back into shape if necessary at this stage, pinned out, pressed again, and left to dry. Pieces worked on a frame will not need such rough treatment. Stranded floss embroidered on Aida or Quaker cloth can be pressed at medium or medium-hot settings on the iron; any piece using synthetics in thread or background fabric should be pressed with a cool iron.

CLEANING

When it comes to washing pieces of embroidery, the current advice is to wash in water as hot as the fabric will stand. Use a mild detergent, thoroughly dissolved in water. If the color runs, separate the item from any other pieces of embroidery, wash it thoroughly (but without rubbing), and rinse it until all trace of the stain disappears.

Never leave the embroidery wet. Remove excess water by rolling the item in a towel and squeezing it gently. Dry it flat; then iron it from the back while it is still damp.

Stitches

CROSS STITCH

The basic stitch used throughout this book (see Fig. 5 and Fig. 6) is cross stitch. There are two ways to work: either make individual crosses, or make half crosses along a line, then return, stitching over the half crosses in the opposite direction. The first method is the most stable and is unlikely to cause the fabric to distort. So it is perhaps preferable if you are working without a frame.

Fig. 5
Cross stitch on Aida.

Fig. 6
Cross stitch on evenweave.

However, as long as you can develop an even tension without pulling the stitch so tightly that it distorts the threads of the fabric, I think either is acceptable. The only absolute rule that applies to cross stitch is to choose which direction your top stitch will go and stick to it; otherwise, the texture will be uneven.

STAB STITCH

In stab stitch, the needle is taken through the fabric from front to back in one movement, then in a second movement taken from back to front. This stitch is used when the fabric is on a frame, or when the material is stiff, as are perforated paper and plastic canvas.

BACKSTITCH

Backstitch is an easy outline stitch, which is used in only a few projects in this book, for example, in some of the Kelmscott designs (page 50). It is usually worked after cross stitch. Bring the needle through the fabric from the back and take a stitch backward. Bring the needle up again at the far end of the next stitch along the line and then take another stitch backward to fill the gap (see Fig. 7). Work over the same unit of fabric — one block or two threads.

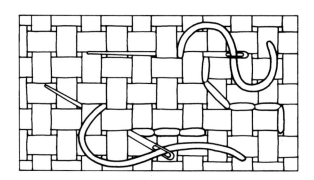

Fig. 7 Backstitch.

HALF CROSS STITCH

This is used for the Flower Pendant (page 41), which is worked on silk gauze, a fabric where each thread is interlocked at each intersection of the weave. It is simply the first half of the cross stitch described above.

PETIT POINT OR TENT STITCH

A variation of half cross stitch, this stitch has to be used when working over one thread of a non-interlocked fabric. In this book, it is used only for the Silver Brooch and St. James

Pendant (pages 41–42), which are worked over one thread of evenweave. It is the same stitch that is used in needlepoint on a non-interlocked canvas. It can be worked diagonally, or in rows (see Fig. 8), and it differs from half cross stitch in having a longer stitch on the back of the fabric than on the front. This is essential for maintaining the stability of the design and the fabric. It is best to work this stitch with the fabric on an embroidery frame.

Fig. 8 Petit Point (evenweave, over one thread).

BUTTONHOLE STITCH

Buttonhole stitch is used to cover a ring for the Jewel Casket (page 37), and in that instance it is worked with gold braid. To make this stitch, take a very long length — about four times what you would normally use. Begin by knotting the braid to the ring. Hold the end of the braid behind the ring and work stitches as in Fig. 9, hiding the end under the stitches. Keep the stitches close together and try to prevent the braid, which is flat, from twisting where it lies over the ring; take the braid through the bottom of the first stitch to complete the twist along the bottom. Carefully thread the end through under the stitches and trim the end invisibly.

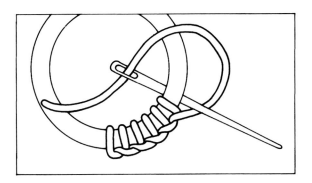

Fig. 9 Buttonhole stitch.

LADDER STITCH

A neat way of joining the edges of two pieces of fabric that have been finished or have hemmed edges is to use ladder stitch. Bring the needle out through the edge at one side and take it straight across into the other edge. Slip the needle through the edge a little way and take a stitch back to the first side, then repeat (Fig. 10). After a few stitches, pull to tighten

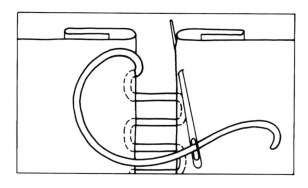

Fig. 10 Ladder stitch.

ANTIQUE HEMSTITCH

Work this stitch on the Larkspur tablecloth and napkins (page 70) for a real heirloom finish, if possible using a thread the same thickness as the thread of the fabric. Decide where the edge of the hem will come and withdraw two or three threads along the length of the piece. Fold the hem so that the turned-under edge just touches the drawn threads and baste in place. Beginning at the left-hand end of the wrong side, bring the thread through from inside the hem, emerging on the wrong side three threads down from the drawn area. Move the needle two threads to the right and surround four of the threads (Fig. 11). Bring the needle back to the right of the clump of threads and insert it between the hem and the front of the fabric, emerging two threads to the right, ready to take another stitch. Pull the thread tight enough to pull the group of threads together. Repeat.

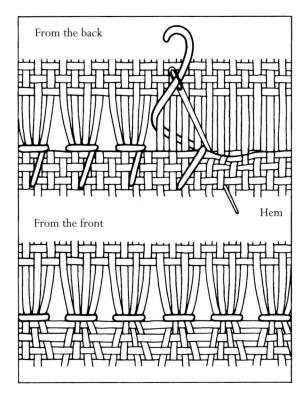

Fig. 11 Antique hemstitch.

Finishing

PICTURES

You can press your work and take it to a framer specializing in embroidery who will do the rest for you. If you prefer to do it yourself, then read on. The method you use will depend on whether or not you want the embroidery framed by a mat inside the frame itself, and on how flat the finished piece of work looks. Whichever choice you

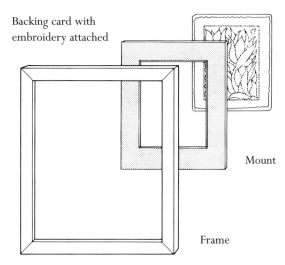

Fig. 12 Framing embroidery with a mat

make, the embroidery will need to be backed by a piece of backing board or stiff cardboard that fits inside the frame.

When using a mat (see Fig. 12), I sometimes just glue the embroidery to the backing board around the extreme edges. I have also used double-sided tape and, occasionally, staples. If you use glue, never put it on an area where it could be seen; it may be invisible when applied, but a stain can develop later. If the piece is to be framed without a mat, it must be laced around the backing board.

Cut the backing board to fit easily inside the frame, remembering to allow for the thickness of fabric pulled around the edge. Mark the center of each side on the back of the board. Mark where you want the center of the embroidery to be with pins at the edges. Lay the front of the board on the wrong side of the fabric, matching the center marks. Fold the fabric around the board and hold it in place by pushing pins through into the edge of the board (see Fig. 13). Start at the centers and work out on opposite sides. Every so often, turn the work over to check that the fabric is held taut and that the grain is straight. When you are satisfied, take a long length of button or linen thread and lace from side to side, pulling the thread tightly enough to hold the fabric firmly in place without bending the board. Repeat this operation with the other two sides. This method is reversible, giving you the option of changing your mind later. I prefer to frame without glass, but you may want to use it. If so, ask the framer not to allow the glass to touch the embroidery, flattening its texture.

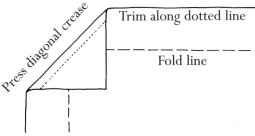

Fig. 13 Lacing embroidery for framing without a mat.

MITERING A CORNER
Mitering is a good way of removing excess fabric from a corner. Fold the fabric along the edges as far as required and mark the fold line. Unfold the turning. At the corner, fold the fabric on the diagonal as shown in Fig 14. Press the crease. Allowing for a small turning along the creased side, trim away the excess fabric. Turn in the long edges, and the creased diagonal sides should meet in a neat miter. Ladder-stitch them together.

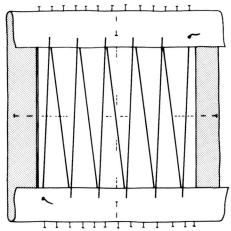

Fig. 14 Mitering a corner.

PILLOWS
On the back of the embroidery, mark exactly where you want the edge of the pillow to be, bearing in mind the sizes of pillow forms available. You will need a pillow form 1in (2.5cm) larger than the finished size. Choose a backing fabric that harmonizes with the embroidered fabric. Cut it to the finished size plus allowances, then pin the fabrics right sides together. Machine stitch following the edge line you marked. Start a short distance from one corner, stitch around three sides, and a little way around the last corner, leaving an opening the form through (see Fig. 15). Work another line of stitching around the corners to reinforce

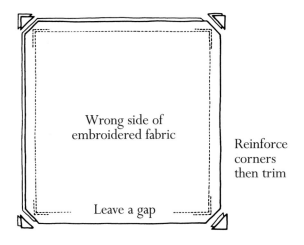

Fig. 15 Making a pillow.

them; then cut diagonally across, quite close to the stitching, and trim the other edges, leaving the usual seam allowance. Turn the pillow right side out and press the seam. Insert the form and ladder-stitch the edges together.

An alternative method is to make the backing piece with a zipper inserted (see Fig. 16). To do this, you need a slightly larger backing piece, cut in half. Place the two halves right sides together. Sew 2in (5cm) of the seam at each end and insert a zipper in the middle opening. Proceed as above, but sew around all four sides.

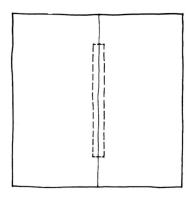

Fig. 16 Backing fabric with zipper inserted.

Open the zipper to turn the cover right side out and insert the pillow form. This method is recommended if you choose to make a round pillow, because it will make a neater edge.

As a final touch, you could add cord around the edges, looped or knotted at the corners. Fringe, which was widely used in the 19th century, can also look attractive.

BOOK COVERS

These instructions apply to the Kelmscott book cover (page 58) and also the Flower Garden checkbook cover and credit card wallet (page 86). The materials are listed in the projects.

Measure from the opening edge of your book around the spine to the other edge. Cut the interfacing to this length, and the same height as the book. Bond it to the back of the embroidery fabric so that it will interline the two covers and the spine (see Fig. 17). Place the embroidery fabric face down on the lining material. You are

going to turn in all the edges to produce a long, neatened strip which you can wrap around, starting from inside the front cover, round the spine, and ending inside the back cover. The finished fabric strip should extend to cover all but $1/2$in (1cm) of the insides. Check this measurement on your book to find the length of the strip and add a little ease at the top and bottom of the height of the book to allow for the thickness of the covers. Baste the embroidery fabric to the lining and machine stitch, leaving a gap at the end of the back section.

Trim the excess fabric and turn right side out. Press the seams and slip stitch the gap. Wrap around the book to check the fit and then ladder-stitch along at the top and bottom to form two pockets for the front and back covers.

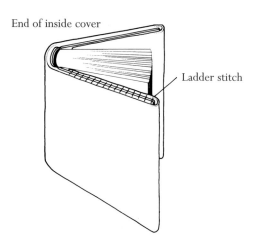

Fig. 18 Wrapping the cover around the book.

Open the book and pull the covers back. Fold the embroidered cover back on itself and slip the book covers into the pockets (see Fig. 18). It should be a tight fit, but not so tight that the book will not close completely.

This method can be used to make all sorts of covers. For greater stiffness, pieces of cardboard can be added to the front and back sections between the embroidered fabric and the lining. That would require additional ease on all seams to allow for the greater thickness.

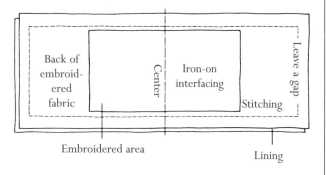

Fig. 17 Making a book cover.

Acknowledgments

This book owes its inspiration to the genius of William Morris, to his magical talent as a designer of patterns, and to the example he set — his determination that he could and would achieve whatever goals he set his mind to, and would achieve them excellently well.

Completing this book would have been impossible without the generous help of many people. My heartfelt thanks to the embroiderers, many of them past or present members of the Winchester Embroiderers' Guild, who have been so generous with their skill and time. I must thank Lizzie Aston for working the Pimpernel Footstool, Laurine Alveyn for the Kennet Dresser Cloth, Barbara Barnes for the Evenlode Tray, Tim Bonner for the Violets Nightgown Bag, Audrey Furnace for the Larkspur Napkins, Sylvia Garnett for the Kelmscott Book Cover, Henry Grey for the Evenlode Coasters, Julie Hazeldon for the Brer Rabbit Picture, Hilary Heatherington for the Flower Garden Glasses Case and Wallet Cover, Kay King for the Violets Pillowcase, Rosie Minors for the Campion and Dove and Rose Pictures, Edith Rackham for the Wild Tulip Tea Cozy and Place mats, Valerie Ray for the Kennet Dresser Set and the Cornflower Picture, Carole Smith for the Kelmscott Photograph Frame, and Paula Tuckey for the Fritillary Picture and the Pomegranate Bowl Lids. A special mention must go to Muriel Grey who stitched the Bird Pillow, the Orange Tree Bellpull, the Flower Garden Checkbook Cover, and the Larkspur Tablecloth, and whose enthusiasm and encouragement have been much appreciated. All have done beautiful work, and I could not have managed without them.

My thanks also to Eleanor Yates for the extended loan of books from her enormous collection, and to Christopher Croft for his computer advice. I am grateful to the descendants of Beatrice for the use of their photo in the Kelmscott frame.

Companies have been very helpful and generous in providing materials and accessories. My thanks to DMC for fabrics and threads and especially to Cara for her advice, to Coats for a variety of threads, to Madeira for an exciting selection of metallics, to Fabric Flair for its evenweave fabrics, to Framecraft for a wide range of accesories, to MacGregor Designs for the footstool, to Ivo Tapestries for the bellpull ends, to Elizabeth Anderson Miniature Embroideries for brooches, to The Sewing Basket for perforated paper, and Craft Creations for cards. Arthur Sanderson and Sons Ltd. kindly supplied fabrics and papers from its current Morris & Co selection to use for the photos.

I would like to thank Cheryl Brown at David & Charles for having confidence in a first-time author, Jane Trollope for all her help, and Brenda Morrison and Maggie Aldred, who have made the book look so attractive. The photographs by Tim and Zöe Hill are marvelous, and Ethan Danielson has done full justice to the designs with his clear color charts.

Finally, I would like to thank my family for all their help and for tolerating the constant tide of charts and embroidery which has filled the house for so long.   —Barbara Hammet

Places to visit

The Victoria and Albert Museum, Cromwell Road, South Kensington, London SW7

The William Morris Gallery, Lloyd Park, Forest Road, London E17

The Fitzwilliam Museum, Cambridge

The Birmingham City Art Gallery

Whitworth Art Gallery, University of Manchester

Kelmscott Manor, Kelmscott, Nr. Lechlade, Gloucestershire (*limited opening in the summer only, but well worth a special visit*)

Standen, East Grinstead, East Sussex (*National Trust – summer only*)

Wightwick Manor, Wolverhampton, West Midlands (*National Trust – summer only*)

Index